Maggie Pie

First Edition

Jasper McCutcheon

Maggie Pie

First Edition

Published by The Nazca Plains Corporation
Las Vegas, Nevada
2007

ISBN: 978-1-887895-98-9

Published by

The Nazca Plains Corporation ®
4640 Paradise Rd, Suite 141
Las Vegas NV 89109-8000

PUBLISHER'S NOTE

Maggie Pie is a work of fiction created wholly by *Jasper McCutcheon's* imagination. All characters are fictional and any resemblance to any persons living or deceased is purely by accident. No portion of this book reflects any real person or events.

Cover Model, Mistress Misty
Cover Photo, Corwin
Art Director, Blake Stephens

Dedication

Dedicated to all soldiers whose bigger battle begins when they get home.

Maggie Pie

Jasper McCutcheon

Contents

Tabled

"Wait here, kids. I'm going to get your mom a couple of Maggies."

Bud Richter parked his car in front of the Koffee Kup Kafe, where inside several farmers had gathered for their daily morning social.

"I just don't understand how it could have happened," said one.

"Our army used to be a force to be reckoned with," said another in his awkwardly-tongued phraseology.

The men were not happy, but at least on this day they had something of interest to discuss besides the weather. The Thursday news was four days old, but they were still talking about it on a Sunday, about the failed rescue attempt of the hostages in Iran. American citizens were still held prisoner. American soldiers died trying to free them.

"It's Carter's fault," one shouted from a back wall corner table, heating the debate.

"That's right," said another. "He's the one who let those dirty Arabs get away with this. God damned rag heads."

Sorrow, anger, and confusion energized the early-day drinkers of coffee and the restaurant where they gathered. Nothing much had changed since its 1938 inception, nor had the town of Holyoke, Colorado where the little eatery was situated. Dotted with square, metal tables made for four, plus three padded booths lining the windows, only upgrades on furnishings and new patterns of tablecloths varied from what had been, that and the topics of discussion on any given morning.

Every day this group of men would pull two tables together, assemble and dawdle, never ordering a meal, never leaving a tip.

"You're all full of shit." Bud Richter silenced their talk. "Is it Carter's fault that Congress killed military funding? Is it Carter's fault that our choppers ran into a sandstorm?"

Nobody dared to answer him. Experience had taught them that their best play was to let him blow off his steam.

Bud was not a member of the morning idler's club. His intention had been to enter, purchase his pies and exit without speaking to anyone other than Maggie Dietrich, wife of the proprietor and finest fruit pie baker in Phillips County. Knowing Bud, the farmers in back should have halted their conversation as soon as they saw him, but the emotions of the event had clouded their judgement. Bud brought them back to reality.

"You knuckleheads always talk out your ass, like you know

something. Stick to your area of expertise... " He altered his voice to a whiny twang and mocked them. "Shore do need rain. Corn's lookin' kinda parched. Heard they got a corter eench over'n Greeley. Shore could use sum here."

Bud turned to Maggie as she dropped his coins of change into his open palm. "Thank you, my dear. Julie's going to be a happy lady."

He had one final bit of advice for the table-sitters. "Talk about your corn, you god damned hayseeds. That's what you know." Bud wiped the sweat from his forehead and made his exit.

One of the farmers pointed to his own temple with his finger, drawing circles while crossing his eyes. And then they all returned to the subject of Iran and the doomed Operation Eagle Claw, after the door had slammed and their antagonist was on the sidewalk.

No farmer he, although Bernhard "Bud" Richter had been groomed for such. It was his father's wish, and his grandfather's wish, but two tours of duty in Viet Nam changed Bud's outlook on things. Bud was a truck driving man -- not a pickup truck driving man, that was for farmers -- Bud Richter drove an eighteen-wheeler for Pearsall Truck Lines based in Cheyenne, Wyoming. Six days on the road, four days off, that was his company-mandated schedule.

The two pies were for Julie Richter, his ex-wife who reclaimed his name after her second attempt for a successful marriage had failed.

Bud's nostrils inhaled a fine mixture of cherry and blackberry aromas as he passed the city limits sign of Holyoke, population 1146. That number would be changing soon. The 1980 census was well under way.

"Well, kids, did we have a blast or what?"

His son, age twelve, answered enthusiastically. "Sure did, dad."

His daughter, age sixteen, preferred to answer as a teenager. "It was all right."

Lisa Richter sat in the front seat holding the paper sack of boxed pies on her lap, while Jackson Richter, Jack, had room to roam in the back seat of Bud's station wagon.

He headed south on the paved State 385 Highway, which would connect him to the unpaved, family-named road leading to his property and home. He no longer lived there full-time, but the valuable acreage was still his by ownership.

Bud had scheduled a week's vacation to coincide with his children's week of spring break from school. Somehow, he had kept them both entertained as they visited him in Cheyenne for five days, which can be stressful for some single men, but not for Bud. Bud adored his kids, not always with the greatest of emotion but certainly with a good portion of his paycheck. They were the one item on his list of accomplishments good and bad for which he made no apologies.

Mid-morning in late April brought air that was crisp and fresh, and after having filled his lungs with Maggie's two still-warm masterpieces, Bud rolled down the driver's side and rear windows on the wagon to alter its interior scents. His 1978 Custom Cruiser was a practical choice for a practical man, or in his words, "What good is a pickup? If I'm gonna haul something I want it covered. No good to have it flapping in the breeze or getting rained on."

Bud, Lisa and Jack were in daydreaming mode, wind and silence preferred to conversation.

In Phillips County, Colorado the two "C's" are king -- corn and cattle. Nestled in the northeast quadrant of the state, its landscape mirrors the best of southwestern Nebraska and northwestern Kansas, if endless miles of flat, monotonous features dotted by sporadic clusters of trees can be considered the best of anything. Rows of newly-planted corn poked from the earth as far as the eye could see, and the movement of Bud's Oldsmobile created vibrating lines of a green-stringed guitar, slithering lines that nearly hypnotized if gazed upon long enough. Passing within proximity of a feedlot where cattle gorged on last season's corn, Bud quickly shut all windows.

"Jesus H. Christ. How can anyone work around that stench?"

Six miles traveled, Bud's house came into view on their left. A speck, that's all it was from here, but the two turrets framing each corner of its front side were unmistakable. He turned onto the gravel road named Richter Road that would lead them to Julie.

Since sunrise, every trail of dust viewed from the kitchen window had caught Julie's attention, but not until the third did she stop what she was doing. She checked the oven. Her biscuits were ready and she removed the sheet filled with one dozen, leaving their fresh-bread aroma on the stove top to permeate the room in cooling. Bud was home, the kids were home, and Julie settled into the swinging and suspended-by-chains bench on the front porch of their house. A tan cloud billowed behind the car, following its pace as though a tumbleweed magnetized to the rear bumper. As Bud turned into the lane, their dusty companion stayed behind. His lane and his circular drive were paved with asphalt, extending off the circle in leading to a two-car garage, separated from the house by thirty feet . No dirt or dust would ever sully the white paint of his structures. He parked in the circle, a few feet past the front porch steps.

"Lookee here, mom." Lisa held up the paper bag.

"Oh, Bud, I can bake too, you know."

Her reaction to his gift was always the same, as was his answer. "I don't want you baking pies. You've got better things to do."

Truth be known, Maggie's crust was airy and flaked, Julie's hard and flat. As for the filling, nobody could touch a Maggie fruit pie for flavor.

"Did you have a good time?"

"Yes, mom." Lisa set pies on the front porch, kissed her mother and headed inside for her room.

"We went to the Black Hills in South Dakota," Jack gave his mother a blow by blow account. "Saw Mount Rushmore and on the way back saw Custer's..."

"Ok, Jack. Give me a kiss and come inside for breakfast. You can tell me all about it."

Bud removed Lisa's and Jack's travel bags from the car, with Elsie, the German Shepherd in charge of protecting his outside property, yapping at his heels and begging for attention. He set the bags onto the porch and gave her what she wanted.

"Hey, girl, give me a kiss." She reared up so he could grab her forelegs while she mercilessly licked his face.

"Oh, Bud," Julie admonished. "Do you like the smell of Elsie's butt-licking tongue?"

"She's the only woman who loves me. Aren't you girl? Yes you are... mmm... kissee kissee."

"You're disgusting. Wipe off that dog spit and let me kiss you."

They did, mouth to mouth, a quick dry-lipped peck.

"Staying for breakfast?"

"And more. Oh, by the way, somebody left a bag of dirty clothes in my car. What should I do with them?"

"Were they soiled by a truck driver?"

"I think so."

"Bring them. I've got nothing else to do."

While Julie took her pies to the kitchen, Bud toted all bags, leaving them in the central foyer of the house. Jack was already at the table helping himself to his mother's biscuits and soon the three of them sat down to scrambled eggs, skillet-fried bacon, stove top brewed coffee for the adults, orange juice for Jack, biscuits, butter and jelly for all.

And for Bud, "I'll have a slice of Maggie blackberry."

Lisa informed her mother that she was going to her friend Martha's house, which would be a one-mile drive in her Bud-purchased Chevy Nova.

"Dinner's at six. Don't forget you have school tomorrow."

"Thanks, mom, I really needed to hear that."

Every detail of vacation was told by Jack, as he ignored his mother's meaningless warnings to not talk with his mouth full.

"Hey, look at this." He crammed half a biscuit into his mouth and ran to his bags, returning with a souvenir. "It's bronze." Jack handed a statue representing Mount Rushmore to his mother.

"Can you name them?"

"Sure. Washington, Jefferson, Lincoln and Roosevelt."

"Which Roosevelt?"

"Teddy, of course."

"Of course."

Jack was finished with adults, deciding to ride the countryside on his Bud-purchased Honda 125 dirt bike.

This left Bud, Julie, Bud's pie and two half-full mugs of coffee alone in the kitchen. Bud poked the pie crust with fork prongs, leveraged a corner piece to his mouth and let the mixture of tart, pastry-surrounded blackberry melt while Julie topped off their mugs.

"Maggie's a pro, that's for sure." He laid the fork onto his platter and handed what was left to her. "Here, you finish it. Want me to wash my spit off of that fork?"

"Bud, please." She lifted his utensil and sniffed it. "Don't you dare." She licked it, pressing her tongue between its Bud-enhanced tines.

"Uh, huh... horny, is ya?"

"Maybe."

"Heard from lick spittle lately?"

"No. Why would I?"

"That's right, you wouldn't. Told you Charlie Hofstra was an asshole. Forgot about you already, huh? He gave up on you faster than I gave up on farming."

"Damn it, Bud. It's been five years. Why do you keep asking me about him?"

"Just checking on my competition."

She lifted a piece of pie towards her mouth. "You don't have any competition, lover boy."

"Gave up trying to find a better man, did ya?"

"Long ago." Julie forked another chunk, offered it to him. Bud took it. "Man, that's good."

"I don't know why mine isn't good enough for you."

"Jealous?"

"Always."

"Well, sweetheart, you're the best in everything else. Just leave the pies to Maggie."

"When are you going back?"

"Tomorrow night. Are you needing a hard dick?"

"Yes. What about Jack?"

"It's a motorcycle. I guess we'll hear it if he comes back... if you don't scream too loud."

"Oh, don't worry. You aren't all that."

"Oh, yes I am. Let's go."

Warm and Hot

Bud's ancestors came from Germany and his parents gave him a German name. Bernhard means bear, and Bud's body type fit the moniker, if he could be a bear standing five feet, ten and a half inches with barreled chest, thick, muscular limbs and sufficient amounts of dark brown fur everywhere other than the top of his head, where thinning exposed his crown.

For Julie's eye, Bud's physique was her ideal. The progression of aging never altered how she saw him. She had never found a suitable replacement. Theirs was a classic relationship of conflict outside the bedroom, harmony in, and Julie led him to the very same bed they had at one time shared in the northeast six-sided turret, with one window centering each side.

"I gotta piss," Bud announced.

'Typical man,' she thought to herself. 'No class,' which was exactly what she needed. Her loins ached as she pulled the covers completely to the floor, removing all obstacles. By the time Bud entered her room, Julie was naked and sprawled in the center of her full-size mattress perched upon antique poster bed.

He found her, enveloped her. Bud's skin was clammy with dried sweat, but soon he warmed to the temperature of the woman beneath him.

Julie clutched her fingertips into the undulating muscles of his back. She inhaled his scent, tasted his spit. Her nipples absorbed the loving tickles of his bear-furred pectorals. Her vaginal walls crushed the massive thickness of his impaling penis. She remembered why she could never be satisfied by any other man. He was her animal, her bear, and he dominated her like a rogue Grizzly of the Great Northwest. Here today, gone tomorrow, but for now Bud was home. Julie clung to him with all her strength.

"I'll be back in a half an hour, Bud."

"Where you going?"

"To put my roast together."

"I better shower."

"Do it before dinner. You smell fine to me."

Jack and Lisa made it for Julie's beef roast, after giving their parents most of the afternoon to wallow in bed, talking for awhile, napping for awhile, making love for awhile.

After dinner and a four-person crew for clean-up, the Richters gathered in the main-floor living room to watch television. Within thirty minutes, Lisa was in her upstairs bedroom on her personal telephone line, and thirty minutes after that Jack was upstairs in his looking over the brochures and souvenirs from his trip. Both were asleep by eleven. Two pieces of Maggie pie and the Denver evening news broadcast later, the television was turned off and all Richters in their beds.

"Julie?" Bud slept in his boxer shorts, Julie in a sheer nightgown. The turret bedroom was painted in a soothing grey of moonlight, as was the man laying on his back with covers folded down to his belly.

"Yes, Bud." She shifted her head from pillow to chest, tickling her nose in his fur, massaging his pectoral with the palm of her hand.

"Think we can have a session tomorrow... after the kids are gone?"

"Have you been a bad boy?"

"I went off on those goof balls at the Kup today. You know, Harold and his cronies."

"What about?"

"About this Iran thing."

"Oh, were they trying to be experts?"

"Of course. You know how they piss me off."

"Sure, Bud. We'll get it all worked out."

Bud's collapsing nasal passages created a faint buzz. She stayed on his chest, listening to his buzz become a roar, until drifting to sleep despite his noises. His snoring had never been a problem for her. Julie hated the silence when Bud wasn't there.

A stairwell off the kitchen led to the basement of the Richter home. Bud opened the door, flipped the light switch and descended the stairs with Julie four steps behind.

They had seen both kids off to their Holyoke schools, mother serving their preferred cereal, toast and juice, father telling them he'd see them for dinner before he returned to Cheyenne. No more early morning bus rides for the Richter kids. Lisa's auto and driving privileges allowed everybody an extra hour of sleep, and even though she didn't like it, her little brother rode with her.

With the children gone, Bud went upstairs while Julie filled the kitchen sink with soapy water. He returned wearing his boxers and open-toed shower sandals. Julie abandoned her cleanup chores.

The underground, dugout foundation of the Richter house ran its full length. Its floor was stone inlaid to mortar, as were its walls. The distance from basement floor to ground-level floors was seven feet. Horizontal, wooden beams supporting the house were spaced twelve feet apart and anchored to the stone walls, while hanging from the center of every other one were flourescent lamps, two-tubed, all of which were lit from Bud's flipping the upstairs switch.

Along the backside wall of the basement were built wooden shelves, which had once housed glass jars of fruits and vegetables canned by Bud's mother, and before her by his grandmother and great-grandmother. Few jars remained.

The shelves were separated by a door which led to a stairwell which led to the back yard, the door long ago having been sealed when Bud unceremoniously hammered a bland sheet of plywood to it's basement-side frame. To further block this door, a three-drawer, metal file cabinet was parked with all three drawers locked. The second series of shelves was used to store Bud's hardware, boxes filled with nails, screws, nuts and bolts of various sizes, each categorized by box and labeled with magic marker. Other boxes contained tapes, vises, clamps, ropes and numerous items that might come in handy for home repair, while one shelf level held nothing but tools electrical and manual -- saws, hammers, screw drivers, drills and any other implement you can imagine that could accumulate in the one-hundred-plus-year existence of this house.

Having stripped to his boxer shorts and shower sandals, Bud passed under the kitchen until he reached the center of the basement, below the main foyer of the house above. To his right was a table, to his left an elevated bench, both built by Bud. He stepped out of his shorts, handed them to Julie and took two paces to his right.

Naked, Bud left his sandals and climbed onto the table.

Clothed, Julie retrieved four spring-loaded metal clamps from a box on Bud's hardware shelf and laid them on the table. In her jeans pocket was a key, which opened a file cabinet drawer containing four ropes, each tied into looped knots of figure eights.

Bud's horizontal table was made of oak wood sanded smooth. It stood twenty-six inches in height. The length was eight feet and width four. He had bored four holes near four corners of its flat surface, and through these holes Julie threaded the ropes, bringing their loops above the surface while leaving their knots below.

He sat in the center of the table, using his hands to slip his feet through the two loops at one end, and then laying flat to reach for two loops at the other end. Bud put his hands through the loops while Julie circled the table. Kneeling beneath, she one by one pulled downward on the ropes and placed a clamp directly below each hole, tightening the loop above. With four clamps in place, Bud was sufficiently bound and stretched spread-eagle to the table's surface.

She stood beside him near his chest.

"How bad?"

"It's a four, Julie." A relatively minor infraction, a level of punishment determined by intensity and by the length of time Bud wished to endure it. Knowing what he wanted, Julie told him, "Goodbye," and she stripped herself naked.

From a box resting on one of his hardware shelves she removed a leather belt once worn by her husband, once brown but now splotched with tan, no sheen to its finish, a width of one inch. Julie clasped the buckled end of the belt into her right-handed grip.

Stretched in four directions, the muscles in his four limbs bulged. His strong belly flattened and every line of power came to life. The beautiful man was now a glorious man-god, and Julie licked her lips.

"What are you going to do to me, woman?" His mighty chest expanded, as he slightly arched his back and lifted his breasts towards her, physically begging her to give her what he so desperately desired.

"Make you pay." She brought the level four brunt of her strength down onto his straining chest. Leather smacked against skin. Arms and legs flexed against the ropes that bound them. His eyes clenched tight and he raised himself further to greet her second blow. She targeted his nipples, tiny brown circles shrinking in diameter, their tips rising to accommodate their shrinking.

Short-breathed, deep-throated grunts and groans followed each taste of leather, as Bud strained every muscle to absorb her blows.

Her third strike whipped into his brown-bushed arm pit; the fourth striking its other-side mate. The fifth landed on his right tit; the sixth on his left. Number seven left a strip of red upon his sternum, just above the pit of his stomach, which is where number eight painted him. Two blows reddened his belly, cris-crossing their lines to form an "X" with his navel as its axis. Because it was her desire, and because it was his, Julie's eleventh and twelfth tastes of leather were given to his tits, causing them to nearly retract into the skin surrounding them.

A dozen blows given, Julie tossed her belt onto the table while Bud collapsed, gasping for air, tiny beads of sweat surfacing on his skin.

"What is it? Why... why are you doing this? What do you want?"

"An apology."

"For what?"

"For embarrassing me in town. I have to live with these people, you know."

"Aw... screw them. They're idiots. It's not my problem."

"Are you going to say you're sorry?"

"No... never."

"Fine."

She picked up the belt and thrashed his legs, whipping the tops of his thighs and knee caps.

"Ugh... god damn you."

"Say you're sorry." She moved onto his shins.

"Fuck them... and you. You will never break me down."

"Really?" She moved to the end of the table, doubled her belt and targeted his right foot.

"Oh, god damn... please... no... not that." His words said no, but his foot said yes. He arched back his toes, opening up the sole of his foot to receive her leather.

"Say it."

"Nahhh, never... don't do this to me."

She shifted her blows to his left foot. He offered it freely.

"Only you can stop your punishment. Apologize to me... NOW!"

"No... I can't... please."

"You will... in time." With the final laying of leather to foot, she stalked to the head end of the table and gently laid her belt on his chest. "Think it over, mister. Try to figure out where I might go next."

Julie Richter sat on the Bud-built bench directly across from him. Also built of wood with padded floor covering draped over and tacked to its flat surface, Bud's bench stood three feet in height. Measuring one foot in width and five in length, today it would remain idle, used only as a place of rest for the dominating female. She caught her breath while he caught his. He stared at the ceiling, his body glistening with sweat, his chest and belly rising and falling at a rapid pace. She stared at him, her furry crotch darkened with juice, her thumbs massaging her nipples.

A level four, four minutes of rest was given. His breathing returned to a normal pace, now drowned out by the steady hum of flourescent lights. He turned his head to look at her, thrust out his lower jaw, filled his lungs with air and exhaled slow and loud, sucking in his belly as flat as it could go. Directly above it, his fully erect peter danced up and down, a thin strand of pre-orgasmic ooze connecting cock head to navel.

She approached him, forming a claw with her right hand. Evil fingers clutched onto his belly, the curved palm of her hand simultaneously pressing the shaft of his penis.

"You are a strong son of a bitch, mister, but I know your weakness."

Her fingers dug deep to his tightened belly muscle. She impaled his hard wall of defense, manipulating muscle as if a clump of dough.

"Ugh... no... you wouldn't."

"Yes, I would and will. But first I've got to get this damned hose of yours out of my way." She let go his belly and found his boxers. Lifting his penis to vertical, she used his waistband to force his hard cock between his thighs, and then tucked the excess fabric beneath his butt cheeks to hold it in place. His tool laid nearly horizontal, pointing to the foot end of the table.

Leather painted his fully-exposed belly, as she repeatedly brought the belt down on him from sternum to pelvis. His arms strained against his ropes. His chest expanded. His middle-section flattened, every line and curve of his abdominal muscles rising to the surface, clearly defined and fully exerted.

"No," he grunted between reddening contact. "Not... my... belly." He gasped for three quick breaths of air, and then flattened again. "I... I can't... take it."

"You will take it... and like it." She climbed onto the table, kneeling between his thighs to resume cris-crossing blows to his belly. With her left hand, she yanked away his boxer restraint, intercepting his cock with her mouth as it sprang upwards.

"No... oh, god no... not that... anything but that."

She tossed aside the belt and clamped her warm mouth onto his thick meat and held it vertical, motionless. Her hands were free, reaching for his chest, fingernails lightly scraping across the tips of his shrunken nipples.

"Naw... please... please don't do this to me."

She formed two fists and pounded his belly with medium-strength jabs.

"Ugh... you evil bitch... ok... ok, I'll say it. I'm sorry."

She took his nipples between fingers and thumbs, twisting them like the knobs of a radio while her mouth orally stroked his penis. Her lips and tongue completely controlled him, her hands busy on his tits. Julie knew only Bud -- not Charlie, not any other man -- only Bud's pecker had been here, and because she loved it so, because his dick nearly drove her insane with lust, Julie's expertise was unmatched. With no apprehensions, she took his penis to the back of her throat while extending her tongue onto his nuts. She crushed his cock head. She wet-scraped his balls, all at the same time.

He shuddered. No other woman could do it. No other woman had ever gifted to him this mind-blowing, simultaneous assault upon his dick and balls, and he cried out with a painfully pleasurable moan of unbridled ecstasy. Bud Richter exploded into her gullet.

His orgasm changed nothing. Despite gobs of male seed streaming down her throat, Julie did not waver, did not alter her pattern of attack. She intensified her crushing strokes upon the head of his penis. She mercilessly tongue-painted his nuts with her spit, while twisting his shrunken tits between her fingers and thumbs. Julie did torture him. Her assault continued long after the poor man had sacrificed his seed to her, until he had repeated his words of apology countless times in agonized groans of post-orgasmic contortions. Julie was no expert. She only knew Bud. With his cock in her mouth, she owned him. He was completely hers, totally vulnerable. With his cock in her mouth, Bud knew he could never truly leave her.

Skull Digging

A phone call interrupted Julie's breakfast-for-two preparations.

"Julie, this is Greg Dietrich at the Kup."

"Oh, hi, Greg. Tell Maggie her pies are delish."

"Thanks, darlin', I sure will. Listen, there's a man here who claims to know Bud. You want me to tell him how to get to your place?"

"Hmm... well, Bud's in the shower... I better ask him what to do. Hold on, Greg."

She started to lay down the phone, but then thought that perhaps a man trying to run a restaurant probably didn't have time to stand by and wait for her answer.

"Greg, go ahead and send him. Probably a truck driving buddy or something. Thanks for letting us know. Bye, Greg."

"No, wait, he says he was in the Navy..."

Julie didn't hear that. She had hung up the phone and was halfway up the staircase.

The bathroom door was never closed when Bud and Julie were the only people in the house. With the shower curtain opened, Bud stood naked reaching for his towel, but Julie grabbed it first.

"Lift your foot." She padded it dry.

Bud stepped over the tub and onto her terry cloth bath mat, and then raised his still-wet foot for her to repeat the process. Julie loved to see him wet, his body hair darkened, his muscled skin aglow. "Are your feet sore?"

"Sore enough to give me a hard on."

"No time for that now. Here." Julie handed over his towel. "Dry yourself. Greg Dietrich called and said a man's coming to see you."

"Oh, yeah... who?"

"Hmm. He didn't say. He wanted to know if he should tell the guy how to get here."

"And you said?"

"Yes."

"But you don't know who it is." It was not a question.

Bud's sarcasm brought an abrupt interruption to fantasies that Julie's naivete no longer brought out the worst of Bud. "Dummy me... I should have asked."

"Yes and probably. When did Greg call?"

"Just now."

"Well, I've got about twenty minutes to fix things. Give me room."

Meaning: get the hell out of my way so I can deal with your lack of common sense. Bud quickly dried and dressed himself in jeans and t-shirt while Julie returned to her kitchen project. He did his best to control his anger, refusing to accept that her gaffe should become anything more than a minor inconvenience.

In the basement, he removed the ropes from his torture table, threw them into the file cabinet, locked it and transferred items from his hardware shelves to the table surface. When finished, the scene of Bud's self-desired punishment was nothing more than a work bench with four corner holes where an overhead light was once mounted. This was the story if anybody ever asked, thought up by him and drilled into her. After making one final walk through the basement, Bud was satisfied that nothing could be interpreted as out of the norm, so he climbed the stairs, turned off the lights and closed the door.

Two cast iron skillets sizzled with Julie's bacon and eggs.

"Well, whoever this guy is, he must have a good nose for good food. You might as well set the table for three, babe."

For Julie, hearing that one word, "babe," was like opening the valve of a pressure cooker. She knew she had done wrong, but unlike most times, this mistake was at least partially fixable.

"Bud, I called Greg and got the guy's name. Herbert Malik."

Five seconds of blank stare brought the name back to Bud's memory. "I'll be god damned. Herbie! One of my old shipmates."

He grabbed a mug and poured himself some coffee. "You done good, Julie." After a kiss to her cheek, Bud took his mug with him to wait on the front porch swinging bench, just as Julie had done for him. Elsie stood guard near Bud's car, and as a black, four-door Mercury turned onto the drive, he called her to the porch.

"Heel, girl... stay."

A dark-complected man stood exactly six feet tall in jeans and checkered cotton shirt. "Bud Richter?"

"Herbie Malik! The New Jersey boy."

Bud stepped off the porch and met his pal with a handshake. "Damn it to hell... it's good to see you." The handshake morphed into a bear hug. "What in the world are you doing in the hinterlands?"

"Well, I told you I'd look you up when we got out."

"Yeah, but you never said it'd be thirteen years and counting."

The two men separated, but kept hands clasped to one another's shoulders for inspection.

"Gosh, Bud, you're looking fit and trim... but what's going on up here?" Herbie rubbed the top of Bud's hair-thinning head.

"It all moved down here." He pointed to his crotch. "You haven't changed a bit. Do you people ever show your age?"

"Not at thirty-eight, god willing."

"Did you drive from Trenton?"

"No, Bud. I got transferred to Denver a couple of months ago. Told myself that I'd find you come vacation time. It's vacation time."

"How long?"

"Two weeks."

"You hungry?"

"You know me... I can always eat."

"Come on. Time to meet my ex-wife."

They stopped on the porch so Bud could introduce Elsie. "She's hell on wheels with trespassers, which you ain't." Bud scratched her back to put her in friendly mode. "It's ok, girl. Say hello to Herbie."

The big German Shepherd lifted off her butt and stood on all fours with tail wagging, inviting Bud's friend to pet her.

"Hello, Elsie." Herbie looked down to avoid eye contact, holding his hand for her to first sniff and then lick. Only then did he pet her.

Julie had slowed her cooking so that everything would be ready for plating when the two men were finished with their reunion.

"Hello, Herbert Malik," she responded to Bud's introduction. "Sit down. We'll talk while we eat."

Julie served. The men took their chairs.

"Had I known you were coming, I'd have told Julie to make you biscuits. All you get now is toaster toast."

"Is that how it works, Julie?" Herbie followed Bud's lead in chomping a slice of finger-held bacon. "Bud barks and you jump?"

"Oh, he barks all the time, Herbert. Sometimes I hear him and sometimes I don't."

"Hey, do you go by Herbert now?" Bud wanted to know. "Or can I still call you Herbie like the old days?"

"These days I go by Herb, but for you Buddy boy, I'll always be Herbie."

"Did you hear that, honey? Only I can call him Herbie."

"Then I'll call him Herb."

"Me, too. We're grown men, now."

"Julie, I'll answer to anything for a woman who can cook like you." Herb forked a chunk of scrambled eggs, which Julie had substituted for fried in order to address her timing issue. She hesitated to banter with him, answering with a polite "thank you" while waiting and hoping that the two men would rehash their Navy days. Herb did sense her reluctance, but unknowingly took Bud in the wrong direction.

"So, this is the beautiful Julie. She waited for you, just like you said she would."

"She didn't have a choice, Herb. I moved her in with my parents."

"No kidding?"

"Yep. Julie's lived in this house since 1963. I graduated high school and left for basic training in Chicago that fall, while she finished her senior year."

"Oh, yeah, I remember that now, Bud."

Julie's apprehension was turning to displeasure, indicated by the fact she had stopped eating. "What else did he tell you back then, Herb? That he went away and left me pregnant at seventeen years of age? Unmarried? That my senior year of high school was a living hell? That I was ostracized by friends and foes alike over the scandal he had left behind for me to deal with?"

"No, sweetheart," Bud smugly answered for Herb. "I never told him that part, but you just did."

Poor Herb could feel the pressure rising, but fortunately was savvy enough to take sides with the woman. "Damn, Bud, you're lucky to still be alive, doing a thing like that to her."

"Think so? Don't worry, she got even. Kicked me out of my own house."

"Oh, Bud. Don't even go there." Julie's tone was tempered with an 'ah shucks' wave of her hand.

"Herb, it's like this." Bud set down his fork and cleared his mouth with a gulp of coffee. "Julie stalked me. Started in junior high school, before I'd even considered what I ought to be doing with my hard dick. She made the cheerleading squad just so she could be around us boys playing football. That was the only thing on my mind, but she was always there until I finally caught on... finally started talking to her. And once she got it through my thick skull, I never looked back."

Julie reached for Bud's hand, eager to hear him recount the tale of her first and only love.

"She was the only girl I ever dated." Lifting her hand in his, Bud pecked hers with a kiss. "Julie took me from boyhood to manhood. From eighth grade on, she was the only thing that mattered to me."

"I still made him play football, though," she interjected. "He was too damned good at it. Besides, watching him knock people around made me love him even more."

"I don't know how we kept from getting pregnant before we did," Bud continued. "I know exactly what night I did her in... a hot August night... got a little careless in a john boat... right out there on that pond." He pointed behind him, which was a wall that showed Herb nothing pond-related.

"He was sweating like a fish. Always has. That does things to me... at least it does when it's his sweat. That's why I didn't make him pull out."

"It was my job to know when to pull out. Not yours."

"Lost in the moment, Herb. That's what we were."

"Saving it up for..." Herb slowly counted his fingers, hoping to extend the atmosphere of nostalgia over tension. "Four years, or longer? No wonder you got carried away that night."

It worked. Man and woman fawned over each other as though they were back in that boat. For several seconds, they both silently relived their junior high and high school years together -- only the good parts, a high-speed, on-screen newsreel of happy days flashing through their thoughts.

"Longer," Bud broke the silence. "Nearly five years." With one final look of love to his one-time sweetheart, Bud released his hand from hers and proceeded to the next chapter of their tale.

"Found out she was pregnant one week after I'd finished basic. I was in Oakland getting ready to ship out. Could have got out of my Navy commitment... maybe, but after a few phone calls to Julie and her parents, and a few more to my parents, we all figured out the best way to handle it."

"Give me that." Julie grabbed Bud's hand. "I like this part."

"That's when we moved her into this house... made it look like I's gonna do the right thing first chance I got. Let my parents take care of her until I could get home to marry her. Of course, I wanted her here so she couldn't run away... didn't want to lose her. And as you can see, it worked. She's still here."

"Little did he know it wasn't necessary." Julie was proud of Bud for what he did back then, and for expertly closing the can of worms she had foolishly opened for him today. "I wasn't going anywhere."

"Now, I can't get rid of her."

With that gap filled, everybody resumed their breakfast consumption and gave their words a rest. Only when three plates were empty and Julie refilled their mugs with coffee did Herb coax them to continue.

"So, Bud, you two must have gotten married after I transferred to the carrier."

"First home leave I got. July 18, 1965."

"And divorced April 7, 1971," Julie added.

"Hey!" Bud puffed up his chest as though insulted. "Thought you said we weren't gonna go there."

"So, Julie," Herb broke in before she could answer. "Was your first child a girl or boy?"

"Oh, a beautiful baby girl... Lisa. She's sixteen now. Got a boy out of him, too. Jack. He's twelve."

"Got pictures?"

"Sure," Bud answered. "Julie, go get one of your albums."

When she returned, the Navy men were finally reminiscing over their Navy days. Herb wisely steered clear of shore leave stories, where Singapore women were readily available and taken by all sailors, including Bud and himself. Instead, Herb told of their boiler room duties together, of how the heat would drench them with sweat, and of how Bud would antagonize him when none of the officers were around.

"That son of a bitch would take off his shoes and socks, hold them up to a vent that shot air down the corridor to me. Nearly gag me with his nasty foot smell."

"Oh, yeah," Bud countered. "You'd do the same thing with your shirt when our stations were reversed. Julie, this fella here has the worst arm pits of anyone I've ever known. Burns the hairs right out of your nostrils."

"Well, you're both clean today... thank god."

Maggie's pie was offered as a finisher, Bud granting Herb the last piece of blackberry while he and Julie cut into the cherry. This and more coffee complemented a page by page description of the Richter kids captured on camera. Julie set the album in the middle of the table above Herb's plate, while she and Bud scooted their chairs closer to sandwich him.

"Lookee, there," Bud pointed. "That was before Jack's first Little League game."

"And there's Lisa ready for her first stint as a cheerleader."

"And that's Jack..." Bud's elbow nudged the corner of the photo album, which knocked Herb's platter off the table, flipping over and into his lap. The piece of pie landed on the navel area of his shirt, while the platter fell to the floor without breaking. Blackberry filling oozed down his shirt, through his belt buckle, along the zipper flap of his jeans and between his thighs as though a puncture wound.

"Jesus Christ, Bud," Julie scolded. "You clumsy oaf."

"Like I said, Bud. You haven't changed."

Julie hand-scraped the mess onto the platter and took it to the sink, returning with damp wash cloth for Herb to clean himself. His technique was sloppy, more of a smearing than a washing. "Hey look, Bud. This blackberry blends right in with burgundy and black plaid."

"You men are such pigs. Here, let me do it."

"For Christ's sake, Julie." Bud waved her off. "Get him another piece and leave him alone."

A slice of cherry was served. "Thank you, madam," Herb tasted a sample. "Hey, Bud, wait until I'm down to a couple of swallows then do it again. Maybe she'll give me another slice."

"You'll eat the whole damn pie if I don't stop you. I remember how you are."

Herb's love of food hadn't changed, but with age his belly had. Rounded just a bit, it extended when seated, slightly hanging softly over his belt line. Herb wasn't grotesquely overweight, just growing into the shape of a man approaching forty, less active than he used to be.

While the slices gradually disappeared, the Richters continued with Herb's photo tour, ending with recent snapshots of Lisa and her new car, Jack and his new motorbike. The book closed, and while Julie took it back to its living room storage area to prevent another accident, Bud asked, "So, Herb, where are you going for vacation?"

"St. Louis, just for a week. Got a sister there."

"You can stay the night here, but I'm leaving for Cheyenne tonight."

"What's there?"

"My job. I drive an eighteen-wheeler."

"You don't farm here?"

"Nope. What are you doing in Denver?"

"Right now I'm working on a case of mysterious skulls."

"Huh?"

"I'm in law enforcement. The GI Bill allowed me to attend Princeton. Got a degree in criminology."

"Skulls? What are you in florensics?"

"Forensics," Herb smartly corrected. "Forensic science. Human skulls have been turning up in back of restaurants. I'm assigned to one in Lincoln, Nebraska, the other in Omaha."

"Oh, a regional thing. You with the Feds?"

"FBI."

Bud smashed crumbs of pie crust into his fork tines, scraped his teeth on metal in transferring them to his mouth.. "Oh...well... I'm proud of you, Herb." He gulped the last of his coffee. "Come on, shipmate. I'll give you a tour of this museum."

From East to Middle

Gerald and Erwin Richter built the house for two families. Two turrets framed two stories. One foyer and staircase centered the original design of two sitting rooms down, six bedrooms up, two kitchens and one grand dining hall down. The entire structure was made from wood cut from trees lining Frenchman's Creek nearly four miles away, the only exception being the ornamental sheaths of metal that topped the pitched roof.

"Some day that damn thing's gonna spring a leak," Bud explained, he and Herb standing off the front porch. "I'll have to get a cherry picker in here 'cause you sure as hell can't walk around on that thing."

The German brothers survived the U.S. Civil War in service of the Union Army, but neither of them desired to resume their pre-war existence working the sweat-shop woolen mills of Lowell, Massachusetts. Their ancestors were farmers and builders. Attracted by free land in Colorado territory already filling with others from the east, many of whom also were of German descent, Gerald and Erwin Richter packed up their families and migrated west.

"Somehow or another, they split up after building this house." Bud's tour ended in the back yard, after having shown Herb the inside (minus the basement) and now the outside of his home. "Nobody knows why, but around 1880 Gerald took his family on to Oregon and Erwin stayed here. He was my great-grandfather. Whatever it was that made 'em split up must have been something terrible."

"Why?"

"According to my great aunt, Erwin's baby sister, Gerald put a curse on this side of the family. Only one son per generation. The rest are all females."

"Is that how it's worked out?"

"Yep. Erwin had one, his son had one, his had me, and I've got Jack. Kind of far-fetched, if you ask me, but it does make for a juicy tale."

A sliver of house-produced shade darkened the green grass of spring, as Herb gazed down a slight slope past barb-wired fence separating the yard from an open field. Geometrically perfect lines of new-corn sprouts were interrupted by a swath of grassland centered by a pool of water, the pond where Lisa was created.

"This field here used to be for cattle. No more of that."

"So, who farms this, Bud?"

"Two fellas. Wilton Chalmers and Mark Dietrich. You know that man you met at the Kup in Holyoke? Mark is his son. Wilton's place is further down Richter Road, over that hill. Mark and Wilton are the new breed, pretty sharp compared to most farmers. Not like those half-wits you probably saw sitting at that back table. Did you see them?"

"Yeah. There was a group of men back there."

"Dawdlers... know-nothings."

"They sure got quiet when I came in. Stranger in town."

"Think they own the place. I don't know why Greg lets 'em sit in there all morning taking up space." He gathered up a wad of spit and squirted a goober to the ground. "Hey, did you see that little stand on their counter with the greeting cards?"

"Yeah."

"Julie makes those. I got her the inks and lithograph stuff. Kinda resurrected one of her high school talents."

"Darn. I'll have to take a better look next time."

Bud was pleased that Herb was considering a next time. "Mark and Wilton must have planted all they want planted here. Julie says they haven't been around since Friday before Easter."

"Do you pay them salary?"

"No. Lease agreement. My land. Their crop. They keep their crop. I get one hundred dollars an acre, and I've got 120 of those here. Another 100 beyond that rise over there." He pointed to the southwest. "They've got that field planted, too. Easy money, eh, Herb?"

"Sure enough. You don't farm at all?"

"Nope. Ain't in my blood. Sold all my dad's equipment after he died. Grand dad built that poor old barn over there... or had it built... can't remember which." He pointed to the white-peeling-to-greyish red behemoth 200 feet off the corner of his house. "Nothing in there now, except for Jack's motor bike. Just an old dinosaur flapping in the breeze."

Herb was fascinated with the towering height and solid build of Bud's barn, but the deterioration of the structure depressed him. Its weary joints leaned a few degrees to the east, slowly losing its battle against countless years of unrelenting, open-field winds. Unlike Bud's well-kept house, the barn to Herb represented abandonment, a way of life left behind and soon forgotten by the only person who could preserve its history.

"Guess I ought to see what Mark and Wilton would want to spiff her up with some fresh paint. Wouldn't help keep her standing any longer. Just make her look pretty when she falls down."

"Why bother." Herb was telling not asking.

"Wanna go in? It's safe for another year or two."

"Nah. I've seen enough."

"Hey, now. Look at me." Bud stood a few feet in front of Herb with palms open and arms extended. "Do I look like a farmer?"

"Could if you wanted to."

"Well, I don't want to. Had my fill of it growing up. We saw the world, man. Chicago, California, Honolulu, Singapore, Tokyo... hell, how could I come back to this? I gotta be on the road... see new things, new people. It ain't like I didn't try, you know. Tried for one year, couldn't take it. Joined the Marines and went back to war in 1969, just to get away from my old man and this."

Herb tried to interject. Bud didn't let him.

"Let me tell you about him. He was a staunch, German son of a bitch. Never showed any affection to my mother, nor me, nor my three sisters. They left as soon as high school was over. Me, I tried to do what I was supposed to do, but nothing I ever did satisfied him. I ain't like that. I would die for my kids. And as far as Jack and Lisa, they're like me. They don't give a shit about this farm. They like new stuff. Motorized. We got Lisa a pony when she was seven. After a couple of weeks she lost all interest. Never rode it, never took care of it. Jack's the same way. They will leave this place first chance they get. Only reason I'm here is because dad left it to me. And when mom dies over there in her Holyoke nursing home, that'll be the end of this Richter relic."

While Bud caught his breath, Herb asked what he wanted to ask earlier. "So let me get this straight. You do four years in the Navy, come back here for one year, and then join the Marines?"

"Sure did. Being on land's a whole different ball game. Got myself up close and personal with the Viet Cong."

"Just to get away from your old man? Kind of a dangerous road to take."

"Yeah, well, gotta do what you gotta do." Bud wrapped an arm around Herb's shoulder and guided him towards the back door." I saw some awful things... did some awful things."

"But you survived it, I guess, unscathed."

"Oh, no I didn't." He opened the screen door and motioned Herb through. "Why, I'm crazy as a loon. Can't you tell?"

To their left was the kitchen where Julie toiled in dinner-making. To their right was the only downstairs bedroom and bathroom, where once the second kitchen had been. Herb was again offered this room to stay the night, "far removed from my girlfriend," as Bud put it, and again Herb declined. He was told, not asked, by Julie that he would be joining them for dinner. He was disappointed when Lisa called to tell her parents that she would be sleeping over at Wilton Chalmers's house, as would Jack, Lisa hooked up with Chalmers daughter Martha and Jack with Chalmers son Brad.

Julie was more upset over this than either of the men, reminding Lisa that her father would be leaving after dinner and the least they could do was to be here when he left, until Bud took the phone from Julie and told his daughter to have a good time. He'd see them all again in about a week.

Their dinner conversation centered mostly on Herb, his college days, his career highlights, and then both men prepared for their separate journeys.

"I'll be back here in six days." Bud and Herb stood near the automobiles after having said their farewells to Julie. "Can you stop on your way back? Maybe get to meet the kids?"

"I doubt it, Bud. Probably drive straight through."

"Well, you've got my number. Don't wait thirteen years this time."

"You've got mine. That highway goes two directions, you know."

A handshake progressed into a hug, and then Bud headed for his car and Herb his. "Go in front of me so you won't eat my dust. When you get to the 385, turn left. It'll take you to I-70 east to St. Louis. Me? I'm turning right, north to Cheyenne."

The westbound Richter Road caught the sun at its worst, centered directly between dashboard and roof, still far enough above the horizon to glare full force. Herb's combination of visor, sunglasses and flattened hand allowed his straining eyes to keep him centered to the flat, uncurved surface, while Bud merely followed Herb's trail of dust.

Upon reaching the paved, two-lane highway, Herb waited for one pickup and one four-door something to pass right to left, and then with a honk of his horn, he turned south, waving his hand out the window to Bud's honk in turning north.

Bud slowly cruised towards Holyoke, and when Herb's Mercury disappeared from his rear view, Bud Richter turned onto a dirt road to reverse directions. "Got one hour to get me another taste of that meaty momma who sleeps in my bed. And the kids are gone, too!"

By the time Bud's wagon parked in the circle drive, Julie was in that bed and waiting.

Long Haul Versus Short

"Where we going, Jenny?"

"Sacramento."

"Sacramento?" Bud placed both palms onto Jenny's desk, shaking his head in feigned disgust. "You know I don't like going west. I wanna go east."

"Fine, mister. You'll have another trailer waiting for you. You do plan on coming back, don't you?"

"Guess I'll have to. At least I won't have to bobtail. Keeps me under one hundred miles per hour." Bobtail meaning tractor without a trailer.

With the other drivers, Jenny was strictly business. With Bud, good-natured bantering was always a part of her dispatch duties. "Nine hundred miles by tomorrow morning. Can you do it?"

"Are you kidding? It's only a thirteen hour trip. What happens when I get there?"

"Meaning, is it a twenty-four hour terminal?"

"Yes, ma'am."

"Sorry, Bud. Your drop-off is, but your pick-up's not."

"An overnighter in Sacramento. Well, fuck me in the ass."

"Oh, I didn't know you liked it there."

"I don't when I'm conscious. What is it that Sacramento needs so bad?"

"Bolts and screws." She handed him his work order. "I know you can handle the screw part. Good luck with the other."

"That's the problem, Jenny. You know me too well."

Jenny Murphy did know him well. She knew he was one of two out of the five long-haul drivers employed by Pearsall who were top-notch professionals. His nine-year record was flawless, never an accident, never a moving violation, log book always returned properly logged, and loads always delivered on time or ahead of schedule.

She also knew both ends of the *screw* part. Jenny had frequented Bud's apartment, the one-bedroom Cheyenne hangout he rented near the Pearsall terminal; the one to which he had arrived an hour later than planned the previous night after having taken advantage of an unexpectedly child-free farm house with one ex-wife needing one more poke. Jenny was married now, but she still remembered Bud's penis, Bud's screw.

As for Jenny's knowledge of the other end of the *screw* part, that involved The Pearsall Truck Line's All-Star Driver, Harry Preston, tops on the seniority list with twenty-two years and counting of perfection. Nobody liked Harry. Everybody was afraid of him -- short-haul and long-haul drivers, dock workers, mechanics, maintenance workers, even the owners tried to avoid him as much as possible. Standing six feet two with a frame as thick as a tractor tire and massive arms to match, Harry's intimidating presence caused his male co-workers to cast their eyes to the floor in his presence. In passing him, they silently prayed to get through the moment without setting him off.

Harry Preston spoke only to Bud, Jenny, and Martina, another dispatcher working the Pearsall terminal. He spoke to Jenny and Martina because he had to, preferring Jenny over the snotty and incompetent (he thought) Martina. He spoke to Bud because they were pals. Teamed together, any man who dared screw with them were screwed over big time by the meaty fists of Harry and Bud.

Within the first week of Bud's hiring, he realized that wherever Harry was everyone else wasn't. Unconcerned, Bud casually spoke to him each time their paths crossed, same as he would to anyone, only to receive a glare of evil as though a mere hello was an invitation to rumble. Bud thought nothing of it. One year removed from horrors seen on the ground in Viet Nam, fear no longer played a part in Bud's response to trouble. "Fuck it," he thought. "Anyone wants to come after me's gonna get my worst, win or lose."

The first words spoken by Harry to Bud came in the break room, where Harry sat alone at a table, munching from a bag of peanut M & M's one unit at a time.

"Hey! You got a cigarette?"

Bud waited until he had deposited his second coin to the coffee machine before facing the man. "No. I don't smoke. Want me to go get you one?"

"Yep."

"You got matches?"

"Yep."

"Here, watch my coffee. I'll be right back." Bud set his paper cup of steaming coffee near Harry's thick fingers and left the break room. On the loading docks, he found a known smoker off-loading a trailer and went for his jacket. "Hey, Jerry!" He held up Jerry's pack of Winstons. "Gonna take these."

"Huh?"

Too late. Bud was gone. He found Harry in the same spot, lips puckered with goober of spit and mucus ready to fire into Bud's coffee if Bud returned empty-handed. "Here you go," Bud palmed the pack for Harry to see. "How many you need?"

Harry swallowed his wad, and then flashed yellow teeth, the first time Bud had seen the man smile. "One'll do. I'm leaving in thirty minutes."

"Me, too." With the Winstons and a quarter returned to Jerry's jacket, Bud and Harry conversed over coffee and candy, while Harry smoked. Turns out Harry was just as intimidated by everyone else as they were by him. He was a brooder, fearful of conversation, fearful of his perceived mental inferiority. And, as long as he was sober, Harry was mostly harmless. His reputation came from the nearby trucker's tavern. That is where any man who dared to interrupt his solitary drinking was sufficiently pounded to meekness. It is also where Bud and Harry became great friends, even though Bud was warned by co-workers when news got around that he and Harry were going for a beer or two.

"Are you nuts? You can't go out drinking with him. He's dangerous. Gonna kill somebody some day. Might be you."

That never happened, although some men who challenged a drinking Harry probably wished they were dead when they woke up. Bud admired this man, three years his senior in age, thirteen years his senior in over-the-road experience. He admired Harry's natural, brutish strength, marveling as Harry proved his claim that he could curl a one hundred ten pound dumb bell thirty times. Sound impossible? Bud thought so, until he brought one with him to the tavern and saw the man do it, boastfully asking Bud which arm he should use before beginning the task.

Harry enjoyed Bud's war stories, like the tale of bloody, bloated corpses floating downstream in the Ben Hai River, men, women and children, while Bud and his Marine buddies casually swam nearby. Just one of many scenes stored in Bud's memory bank that were shared with Harry, along with Bud's take on things derived from these experiences.

Bud's new pal soon adopted Bud's philosophy that it's a waste of time to give a damn about what anyone might think of him. Every man has his strong points and weak points for good reason, and no man need apologize for any of it. Some use brain; some use brawn; some use both, but as far as Bud and Harry were concerned, any man stupid enough to stir shit in a trucker's tavern deserved whatever justice was dealt to them. Bud and Harry enjoyed their reputation, which in fact kept them out of trouble far more often than getting them into it.

There were exceptions to this, of course, and Jenny Murphy just happened to be in the tavern for one of these events with her husband

George in tow. The challenger? Chuck Hicks, who had the audacity to go by the name Chuckie. He was a new Pearsall hire, short-haul driver, who upon hearing of Harry's and Bud's badness, decided to cut them down a peg -- he and his five, inbred-looking companions.

Of the five, Chuckie possessed the features most difficult for the eye to tolerate. Short and wiry, with oily skin and overlapped teeth that went every direction but straight, Chuckie had devoted his life to being a pestering punk and done so successfully.

After Chuckie and friends ordered and received their bottles of beer, they turned to stare down the only other patrons, a foursome gathered around their favorite table near a coin-operated juke box, inactive at the moment.

"So, that must be the hot shots," Chuckie taunted loudly. "Big, bad, Harry and his goofy sidekick, Bud."

While Jenny and her husband tensed, Bud and Harry looked at one another. "Oh, shit. Here we go again."

One of Chuckie's backups fueled the fire. "Who's the other two? They here to protect 'em?"

"One's their whore and the other their bitch," Chuckie answered. "The four of 'em better get the hell out of here. This is MY bar, now. No room for pussies."

Bud spoke softly to Harry. "Wanna use the skedaddle strategy?"

"Sounds like a winner, Bud."

"You two stay here," Bud instructed Jenny and her other half. "We'll be right back."

Bud and Harry casually rose from their chairs with apologies. "Gee, we're sorry, mister," Bud whined. "We didn't know this was your place."

"Yeah, our mistake. We'll just leave it to you, nice and quiet. No harm done," Harry reasoned. He and Bud cautiously stepped towards the door, attempting a straight line exit while keeping eyes glued to their antagonists.

They bolted, immediately turning left in a sprint around one corner and then two. In the back of the tavern they stopped, surprised that none of the six was in hot pursuit -- a testament to their slow-working brains, causing a delay that worked much to Harry and Bud's advantage. The extra fifteen seconds allowed them to maneuver a wheeled dumpster to the corner of the building, and when the first man in the line of pursuit cleared that corner, Bud and Harry rammed him with hard metal, bouncing him into the parking lot while the next two crashed into the container's side. Like Keystone Cops, the other three accordioned into the first two, all five dazed and immediately pummeled by flying fists.

40

Those men never recovered from that collision, never gained an advantage, even when the sixth man returned from the parking lot to join the fray. Harry was a hurricane. For him, anything that could possibly be used as a weapon was used -- feet, hands, head, teeth, bottles, cans, and any other handy item that might be laying around. Bud took a more scientific approach, utilizing his boxing skills learned while in the Navy. His efficient left jab kept a man at bay, followed by his left hook under a man's wild and wide right, which is what most *tough guys* always throw because they don't know anything else.

A ten-minute rumble, two against six, resulted in four laying prone in a state of semi-consciousness, with two more staggering towards their automobiles, hands clasped to bloody, broken and cut facial skin in an attempt to keep it from flopping around. George Murphy joined in for mop up, after the need had passed and with Jenny standing nearby. After all, those men had insulted his wife. With Chuckie Hicks struggling to regain his feet, George kicked him in the rib cage to send him rolling. Justice served, a wife's honor restored.

"Guess that'll do it, eh Bud?"

"Guess so, Harry. Are you hurt?"

"I dunno... let me look." Harry scanned from his feet upwards, and then inspected his hands. "Damn! Ripped one of my nails. What about you?"

"Must've cut my knuckle on some gnarly teeth. Chuckie's, I suspect. Everything else looks good."

And so, the sterling record of Harry and Bud remained intact. They never bothered admonishing the four men who remained on the pavement. No words were necessary. Bud, Harry, George and Jenny nonchalantly returned to their table, where the Murphys ordered another round of drinks.

Chuckie Hicks did manage to show up for his next shift. Purple eye sockets and cheek bones, cut lip, missing tooth (no great loss), and scratches to face, neck and arms merely worsened his already unpleasant appearance. He was humbled, but only in the presence of Bud, Harry or Jenny. His bruised ribs reminded him that she deserved his respect. For everyone else, he remained a mouthy pain in the ass.

With work order in hand, Bud wrapped up his conversation with Jenny. "How long?"

"Trailer's ready. They're bringing your cab now. Seven-thirty, you're out of here."

"Ok, slave driver." Positioned nearby, a giant, restaurant-style coffee maker provided the brew to fill his thermos, and with that done Jenny handed over his packet filled with invoices, bills of lading, and permits needed for each state through which he would travel. "Here, you forgot this."

"How could I? By the way, where's Harry?"

"On his way to Detroit. Out at seven. Why? Can't you function without him?"

"He's a dangerous man, Jenny. You know that. Somebody's got to keep track of him."

"You two aren't half as dangerous as you think."

"Oh, lady... if you only knew."

"I do know, Bud. Be careful out there. Have a safe trip."

The Lincoln Highway

In the break room, Bud sat alone waiting to hear his name on the intercom. He checked his watch, synchronized it with the clock on the wall that read 07:27 plus thirty-four seconds. The clicking of the second hand meshed with low hums of vending machine lights, as Bud impatiently tapped his fingers on the packet of paperwork laying on the table in front of him. Quirks and particular methods had been developed over the years. He never opened his packet until in the cab of his truck. One cup of vending machine coffee would go with him whether he had finished the coffee or not. Crunched and tossed to the passenger-side floorboard, this cup was his good luck charm reminder of his home base, from Pearsall Truck Lines to Bud Richter.

Pearsall colors were blue and grey, Bud's work attire consisting of the company-provided shirt, light grey button-up with dark blue pinstripes and the Pearsall emblem, oval white background with dark blue Pearsall script. Five more were folded and packed in his duffel, along with ample supply of his own blue jeans, socks and underwear.

Bud Richter, Bay Seven came the familiar female voice of his favorite dispatcher, Jenny, and Bud stuffed his thermos, log book and paperwork into his duffel bag, grabbed his empty cup and exited the break room.

"Good morning, Jimmy."

"Lookee here, Bud. A brand spanking new 1980 Freightliner, just for you."

"Oh, yeah. I heard these were coming." Bud had to shout in order to be heard over the rumbling of diesel motor. Factory paint identified the tractor's ownership, all sky-blue with Pearsall logos on each door of grey oval background and blue script. The shine of new tractor contrasted sharply to the generic trailer, its dull, cold grey metal interrupted by black, five-inch-tall, stick-on lettering at the upper corners and both doors to designate its statistics and identification. Bud inspected his new ride. "She's a beauty. Gonna miss Matilda, though."

"Time marches on, Bud," Jimmy shouted back. "Those Kenworths served us well, but these will eventually replace all of them. First two arrived Monday. Harry took the other one out earlier this morning."

"Oh, so the senior drivers get to be the guinea pigs. I get it."

"You mean lucky ducks. Here, I brought something for you."

"What's this?"

"Tape."

"Cassette? Oh, shit, don't tell me. No eight-track player? All I brought with me's eight-tracks."

"That's why I got you this."

"Let me see. Six Days on the Road and Other Trucker Favorites."

"Yep. Got your favorite song on there."

"Why, I oughtta kiss you. Wait... which recording is it... 1963... damn, this little shit is hard to read... Dave Dudley... Golden Wing Records... that's it! Jimmy, I will kiss you."

"You can kiss my ass and nothing else. Hope you like your one tape. It's that or the radio."

With Jimmy already having opened the door, Bud stepped up into the cab, tossing his duffel on the passenger seat and settling into his. "Mmm... comfy." He took out and opened his packet, distributing his paperwork onto dash-mounted clips. "Jimmy, thanks for the tape. I'll probably have it worn out by the time I get back."

"You keep it. Start a new collection."

As Jimmy moved on to his next assignment, Bud grabbed his gloves and exited the cab for a walk-around inspection. Jimmy had already pulled the rig several feet away from the dock, leaving the trailer open for Bud to secure. He checked the driver-side tires, closed the doors and locked the latch, walked the right-side tires, checked the hose and wire connections from cab to trailer, circled the front of the tractor and returned to his driver's seat. With a close of the door Bud strapped himself to the seat, ground his new Freightliner into gear and eased away from the loading dock. A required stop at the exit gate allowed Bud time to familiarize himself with the gauges, air brakes, mirrors, switches and gadgets, while an inspection man walked around Bud's rig one final time.

"Lights are good. You're good. Have a safe trip, Bud."

"Thanks, Wally. See you in six." Bud reached down to take the inspection ticket from him, clipping it to the dashboard of Matilda Two, a temporary moniker thought up by Bud until he could come up with something better.

Pearsall Terminal cleared, he turned west onto Lincolnway, keeping in the right lane at legal speed. Three miles of thirty-five-mile-per-hour surface street interspersed with traffic lights, the Lincolnway took him past the southern edge of Warren Air Force Base before filtering him onto Interstate 80. By the time he reached it, Bud felt as though he and Matilda Two were old friends.

In Cheyenne, the Lincolnway is named for what once was but is no more -- the Lincoln Highway, the first coast-to-coast throughway ever to exist in the United States. Officially opened in 1913, the two-lane, paved highway began in Times Square, New York City and ended in Oakland, California, where, with the famous Oakland Bay Bridge still 26 years in the future, these motorists were carted by ferry across the bay to San Francisco, thus completing their twelve-state, 3390-mile trip.

Interstate 80 replaced the Lincoln Highway to become the first uninterrupted coast-to-coast, non-stop highway in the country, with four lanes closely following the original path of two. "Every now and then, you can see the old pavement," Harry had told him. "Look for it, Bud. There's ghosts out there. They're watching us, making sure we're ok, keeping us on our toes."

Bud rarely contemplated the possible existence of spirits good or bad, but pretty much figured that like religion and other philosophies of the unknown, it's safer to err on the side of believing in something that doesn't exist, rather than scoffing at something that does. After all, prior to his on-the-road life, he had on many occasions summoned supernatural help in times of danger as we all have, verbally, whether we believe in such things or not. Bud usually came out of such predicaments in good shape, so whenever he was driving the endless miles on Interstate 80, Bud looked for the old highway in case danger was waiting up ahead, just to let those friendly spirits know he was thinking of them.

With forty-five feet of boxed bolts and screws behind him, Bud traveled west along steady concrete covering mostly flat terrain. The further from Cheyenne and Laramie, the thinner the traffic. His new Freightliner was smooth, both the sound of the engine and feel beneath him. A comforting hum buzzed his ears and his butt. He preferred this atmosphere to music, as he scanned the pale green grasslands interrupted by two strips of highway, the early morning sun occasionally flashing in his side mirror.

He limited his liquids, usually coffee, to small amounts when driving, but still was prepared for the inevitable need to evacuate. To do this without a time-consuming stop, he brought along a wide-mouthed glass bottle once filled with orange juice, now rinsed and dried and ready to receive fluid from his bladder. He reached into his duffel bag for the container, removed its metal lid and unzipped his jeans. Perfect angle and perfect fit, a healthy flow of processed Cheyenne coffee streamed down the neck to the bottom of the glass.

Bud was on a slow climb, heading for the continental divide past Rawlins and rising from four thousand to seven thousand feet of elevation in the process. Behind him, all rivers flowed east; before him, west. Once that little landmark was passed, there was little of interest for the next hundred miles, and within minutes of passing Rock Springs Bud's eyelids began to droop. The calm of the Freightliner was too good for Bud's own good, so he opened the cassette case and removed the cartridge. "Let me see," he said to no one. "Which way does this damn thing go?" He held it one way then flipped it over. "That's it. Like a miniature reel-to-reel tape." He pushed in the tape. Nothing. "You might wanna turn it on, dumb ass." He pushed the radio knob.

An aggressive, plucking electrical guitar blasted out Bud's favorite song much too loudly, scaring away any temptations of further drowsiness. "Shit!" He found the volume button and made his adjustment, cracked the driver-side window for cool air and enjoyed the adrenaline-pumping atmosphere he had created. Dave Dudley's macho but smooth voice recounted a six-day haul coming to an end, while Bud and his new Freightliner's five-day round-trip haul kicked into overdrive.

Slight, but lengthy inclines and declines alternated the miles away, leading Bud to the Green River Tunnels. Deep below him in prehistoric lake beds unnoticed from the highway, mining operations extracted the mineral trona, used to produce glass, detergent and baking soda.

"Well, Matilda Two, time to test your tranny." Bud took out a packet of chewing gum from his duffel to prepare his ears for the Three Sisters. This mountain range features three major up and three major down grades, their severities cause for a third trucker lane of concrete. This gave Bud plenty to do, as he constantly downshifted to accommodate loss of momentum on upgrades, upshifted at the peaks to let gravity rebuild speed, and then resumed downshifting to assist his air brakes in preventing a gravity-induced, downhill runaway. "Hey, M-Two, you're a little rough. No sweat. I'll have you good and broken in before this trip is done."

By the time he crested the third peak, Bud was perched at nearly seventy-five hundred feet above sea level, chomping vigorously on his gum to relieve the altitude pressure in his head, and ready to relax while I-80 gently graded him towards Evanston, the end of Wyoming.

As was always the case, Bud's entering Utah shifted his attitude from enthusiasm to loathing. No music could help him here. He hated Utah. "Damnedest place I've ever seen," he'd say. "Everything is backwards. Like a foreign country."

First stop of the day, Utah Port of Entry. Bud exited the highway, relieved to see only two trucks in line ahead of him. He ejected the tape and turned off the radio, edging his truck forward to become second in line. On the scales, the Pearsall trailer passed visual and weight inspection, all paperwork was in order and Bud was sent on his way after a thirty-minute ordeal. No complaints. Just part of the job. He parked in the large open area beyond the scales provided for visual inspection and did a walk around, mainly for the trailer tires and brakes. Once back on the interstate and up to speed, back into the radio went his music tape. "Ah, I'm sick of truck songs. Wish I could play my tapes. Let it go... see what else is on here. All right, Jimmy Martin. That's more like it."

The next mileage sign showed Salt Lake fifty-one miles ahead. Echo Canyon would soon define the landscape with more steep ups and downs, the downs outnumbering the ups. Brightly colored red rock walled the highway to Bud's right, as he downshifted once more, evenly distributing the work load between his brakes and engine drag to maintain his speed control. Twenty-five miles out of Salt Lake City is all decline, dropping from nearly fifty-five hundred to less than forty-three hundred feet. At Lamb Canyon, a beginning series of left-lane runaway truck exits are provided and Bud downshifted another gear to put a drag on his downhill momentum, or at least that was the idea.

A heart-wrenching grind vibrated every surface of his cab. He tried to go back to his previous gear. Same result. More brake pressure was applied, as Bud frantically searched for any gear that would take. Useless, and the loaded trailer behind him pushed his speed over seventy miles per hour. Things were heating up. He signaled left, drifted to the left lane, while forty-nine thousand pounds coasted freely down a six-degree grade. Constantly pumping pressure on heated brake pads reduced their effect. Wisps of smoke began trailing from his wheels. No gear could be found and automobiles were less than an eighth of a mile in front of him, their distance quickly disappearing as Bud's speed passed eighty miles per hour. He laid on the horn, praying the motorists in front of him would react and move aside, praying for the runaway exit to appear, praying for his transmission to accept any gear.

"Where the hell is the ramp? Come on, you son a bitch... shift." He repeatedly pumped the clutch, disengaging in hopes that reactivation would unlock the transmission. "Brand new fucking piece of shit... give me a gear." The grind of locked transmission was deafening. The squeal of burning brakes was worse, but not enough to drown out the final song on his tape, Red Sovine's *Teddy Bear.* "Oh, Christ. I hate that fucking song. Little crippled punk. Bugging everybody on the CB with his GOD DAMNED MOTHER FUCKIN' PROBLEMS!"

The screamed expletives directed at the song, but not caused by the song, ended Bud's controlled thoughts.

His pulse reached the maximum a healthy heart can tolerate; his actions instinctual, in survival mode; his speech to himself.

Where's my ramp? Quarter mile. Hurry up, you son of a bitch. Get out of the way! (steady blast of air horn). Fucking idiots. Let me die alone. Come on. Take a gear, you whore. Get outta the way. Are you deaf? He ain't moving. Gonna ram him. Outta time. Gotta leave the highway... no... there's the ramp... I can get there (pedal stomped and pumped with all his strength). Close enough... NOW! (wheel turned left, tires screeching, red-hot brakes smoking). Steady... stay with me... Ok... Just you and me, you broken bitch. I'm taking you with me. Come... on... you... mother... fucker... CATCH!

Bud had no clue as to what gear he hit, but didn't care. He released his clutch pedal and the sudden drag jolted him towards the windshield. Safety straps held firm. Both hands clasped to the wheel. Brakes applied full force. Bud struggled to control his rig, as transmission teeth broke into a thousand pieces. A cacophonous symphony of under-the-hood destruction, of clanking and twisting metal counterpointed with the screaming of brakes and screeching of smoke-billowing tires. Brand new transmission obliterated itself, holding gear long enough until whatever was left of the brakes could bring forty-nine-thousand pounds, and Bud, to a halt.

No time for celebration, he shut down the motor, unstrapped his body. He grabbed a fire extinguisher mounted on the panel behind his seat, exited the cab and looked for flames. None on the tractor tires, plenty on the trailer's left. Bud sprinted to the back of the trailer, pulled the pin, aimed the spout and squeezed the trigger until flames on rubber subsided to smoke. He circled the trailer's rear. Inner right tire aflame. He emptied the cannister to extinguish that threat before running to inspect the right side of the tractor, where all was hot, but good.

And then, Bud Richter was finally allowed to draw a deep breath of air.

Standing on the passenger side, he looked to his right. The wooden blocking board, twelve feet tall by twelve feet wide, held upright by two heavy iron brackets buried deep into pavement, the stopper to which his eyes had been frozen, the one through which he had fully expected to crash, stood untouched less than three feet from the front of his bumper.

He bent to one knee and looked under the tractor. What was left of a transmission laid on the pavement, wisps of smoke enveloping mangled metal.

Walking the length of trailer, he eyed beneath it strewn pieces of metal framed by intermittent lines of black tire tread. The line of broken transmission parts extended behind the trailer and back a healthy distance towards the entrance of runaway ramp.

Bud continued his stroll, retracing his path until the metal was no more. Here is where that foul transmission had decided to finally take a gear and destroy itself, but at this spot in the road something else was different, too. It took Bud awhile to decipher it. The ramp was wider, but not the asphalt. Underneath, slightly extended on both sides of asphalt, red bricks.

Bud Richter fell to his hands and knees to kiss these red bricks. The Lincoln Highway. What once was will never be forgotten.

Men at Work

Bud was no fan of the CB radio. The endless chatter strained his nerves when driving, but he would use it for information when hazardous weather was about. Otherwise, channel nine for background noise is where he left it. That's the channel for emergencies and for motorists who need assistance or information, which Bud happened to be. His call for help was relayed by truckers to the State Patrol, which brought a Utah Trooper to Bud's runaway ramp location in about fifteen minutes. Following close behind was a fire crew, who efficiently doused all that still smouldered.

"Are you all right?"

"Yes, sir. Not a scratch." Bud handed the patrolman his license and extended his hand. "I'm Bud Richter, Pearsall Truck Lines out of Cheyenne, Wyoming."

"Paul Henderson, Utah State Patrol." He took the license with his left hand and shook Bud's with his right. "What happened?"

Bud told the short version, knowing the detailed version would be repeated for Trooper Henderson's report. After receiving an all clear from the Fire Captain, Henderson inspected all stickers and permits in Bud's cab, and then scrutinized his work orders and contents of his invoice packet, as the fire pumper left the ramp.

"Must have been quite a ride."

"Yes, sir, it was. You can see the trail of engine parts all the way back there."

"And tire marks."

Bud made no comment on the ironic place where his salvation began, figuring that if Trooper Henderson happened to be Mormon he wouldn't care to hear of such silliness as ghosts and dead-trucker interventions.

"Come with me, Mr. Richter. I'll get you hooked up with your company."

After reporting on his radio that all was clear, Trooper Henderson requested his dispatcher call Bud's company, reading the number off of the work order with Bud sitting next to him in the passenger seat.

"Pearsall Truck Lines."

"This is Trooper Paul Henderson of the Utah State Patrol. One of your drivers has had an accident. He is uninjured. His name is Bud Richter and I will let you speak with him." He handed the speaker to Bud.

"Martina? This is..."

"Bud, are you ok? What happened? What..."

"Yes, I'm fine. Is Jenny there?" Bud was embarrassed by his dispatcher's lack of professionalism in the patrolman's presence.

"No. Where are you? How did..."

"Martina... stop. Put me through to Mr. Jacobs... or anybody who's in the office." *Ding bat,* he thought. Covering the mouthpiece, Bud turned to Henderson. "Woman's too excitable to do me any good."

Henderson nodded in agreement.

A twenty-second delay landed Jacobs. "Perry, this is Bud Richter. I've had a self-involved accident. No injury to me or any other persons. Unit B1247, bound for Sacramento, is out of commission."

"One moment, Bud. I'll take down your information."

Glancing to Henderson, Bud smiled with a thumb-up of approval. "Ok. Go."

"Unit is on westbound I-80; runaway ramp off the left lane just past Exit 137a, about six miles east of Salt Lake City." Bud hesitated while listening to Perry's fingers peck the typewriter, thankful for Perry's typing rather than writing by hand. "Unit is upright; cab's transmission destroyed; other engine damage possible; trailer's brakes and tires severely damaged."

After a slight delay, Perry came back. "Bud, do you wish to complete the delivery or come home?"

"I'll complete delivery."

"Can you access your cab?"

"Yes."

"Can the semi-trailer and tractor be moved together?"

Bud looked out the patrol car's windows, where steep declines began within ten feet on both sides of the ramp asphalt. "Doubtful. No room to turn it."

"Stay with your unit. Tune your CB radio to channel 47. Representative from BXM Transportation will contact you with further instructions."

"Thank you, Perry. Will do. Anything else?"

"Not now. Does the officer need to speak with me?"

Trooper Henderson took the speaker mic from Bud. "This is Paul Henderson, Utah State Patrol. Will take information from Mr. Richter and contact your company if needed."

"Thank you, sir. My name is Perry Jacobs. My direct phone number 307..."

With the patrol car angled to the left of Bud's tractor cab, Bud climbed into his unit to open channel 47 at high volume, and then returned to Trooper Henderson's passenger seat. Midway through the information gathering for Henderson's official report a man's voice blared from Bud's CB. "Break for driver of Pearsall unit B1247."

With Henderson's permission, Bud climbed into the Freightliner cab. "Pearsall B1247 here. Go ahead."

"Towing units are in route from BXM Transport Leasing. Estimate arrival within an hour. Ride with one of our drivers to our terminal."

"Will do. Thank you. Out."

Paul Henderson stayed with Bud until the BXM people arrived, as the two men took another walking tour of the damage. "Hard to believe a brand new tractor would lock up on you like that, Bud."

"Yes, sir." It was a relief for Bud to hear the law man drop the formalities of *Mr. Richter*. His fears of Trooper Henderson's possible skepticism regarding events as told were allayed. "Exactly what I was thinking when I's trying to jam it into gear."

"Bet you were thinking all sorts of things."

"No doubt. Half of which I don't remember." Bud stared at the tractor, not thinking about the tractor. He threaded his fingertips through his thinning hair while reflecting on both his good fortune and that of other motorists."Oh, well, so much for my perfect driving record," Bud flippantly remarked, as though this were important to him. Before the accident, Bud's record had been a badge of honor for him, as it is for most commercial drivers, but that seemed trivial now. All humans were alive, including Bud. As for the unit, tough cookies.

"I'd say this will look good on your resume, Bud. Considering what you were dealing with, seems to me you're a darn good driver."

"Thank you, sir."

"Paul."

"Paul."

"Every man's got protectors, Bud. Some have more power than others."

"True. I think the more you believe in 'em the stronger they are."

Henderson's upturned lips and thoughtful stare conveyed agreement, and Bud prepared to hear a sermon regarding some specific prepare-for-the-afterlife genre, most likely Jesus, but got instead a light touch of fist to shoulder. "Come on, Bud, help me measure these skid marks. What size shoe do you wear?"

"Nine and a half."

They did it by walking, Bud along the trail of left tire tread and Paul on the right, both men remembering their number and moving aside when the tow truck entered their ramp. Bud thought this a rather unusual method for determining the length of skid marks. No tape measure? No fold-out yard sticks? Hell, why not just visually estimate for now? The insurance adjusters would be collecting exact data, probably within hours.

"Got one hundred eight here, Bud. What've you got?"

Bud wasn't finished on his longer trail with shorter feet. "Hold on... one twenty-three."

"One helluva ride, Bud. Controlled like a pro."

"Didn't feel controlled when I's doing it." Bud's comfort with this man increased upon hearing the word 'helluva'. Not likely that Paul's spiritual beliefs were guided by any conservative *you can't do this and you can't say that* theories. Henderson didn't write down those numbers. It was busy work. His purpose was to keep Bud occupied until the rescuers arrived, to keep his brain from rehashing the event, or worse yet, from altering the script of his event with the usual "what ifs" that can cause a man to question himself. Henderson was protecting Bud from dwelling on imaginary scenarios of his own failures, of disasters that might have occurred but did not, and therefore should not be entertained. Paul Henderson had seen it countless times, the tricks played by a recently-traumatized brain, and so he thoughtfully guided Bud through his vulnerable time of waiting.

Within minutes of the towing unit's arrival, a Peterbilt hostler tractor, designed and used for maneuvering trailers within the confines of a truck terminal, pulled into the ramp. Two take-charge men inspected their challenge, while Bud and Paul made their way back towards Bud's unit. One of the men was known to the patrolman.

"Hello, Jack."

"Hello, Paul. Is this our driver?"

"Bud Richter, Jack Morton."

"Pleasure. Lost your tranny, huh?"

"Every tooth. Saved me from crashing that barrier, though."

"What's the plan, Jack?" Paul kept things moving.

"Well, we're going to break them down. Tommy will move the Freightliner to the side out of the way. Insurance adjusters want us to leave it here. I'm taking the trailer to our terminal."

"You going to need lanes?"

"Just the lane for the ramp. I'm gonna back us out of here." He turned to Bud with a smile. "Hope no more trucks come along with your problem. Won't lift their spirits much to see the runaway ramp closed off."

Paul radioed his dispatcher for the highway department to close off the ramp, while Tommy lowered the legs of the trailer.

"Bud, you stay with them. I'm going to take my patrol car up towards the entrance."

"You can help me, Bud," Jack added to the instructions. "Let's unhook your air." They climbed between tractor and trailer to disconnect all hoses and electrical wires. "Get what you need out of the Freightliner and put it in Tommy's tow truck."

After dumping the contents of his piss jar, Bud threw it in his duffel bag, taking it along with his paperwork and cassette tape. He turned off the CB, climbed down and circled in front of the Freightliner, where Tommy laid on the ground hooking chains to its undercarriage.

"How you been, Bud Richter?" Tommy looked up grinning ear to ear.

"Damn, Tommy. It's good to see you."

"Yes, sir. I'll catch you at the terminal. Tell you all about it."

Bud's statement couldn't begin to summarize his true joy in seeing Tommy, for he had lost track of Tommy Haynes. Seeing Tommy safe and secure in a good-paying job represented a Bud Richter success story.

Prior to this moment, Bud's last sighting of Tommy had come on a cold January night in 1978, outside a Salt Lake City truck stop. There, between rows of idling tractor engines, with down-time drivers sleeping inside the bunks of their cabs, Tommy Haynes moved from door to door, hustling for cash, or food, or anything of value, with no coat and no front teeth. Bud spotted him working the aisles, knocking on doors, just as Bud was himself preparing to bunk down for a few hours inside Matilda, the Kenworth.

"Tommy?" Bud didn't shout from rolled down window, but left his cab and moved towards the young man.

There was no answer. He stood frozen, waiting for the trucker to come close.

"It's me... Bud Richter."

"Yeah? Oh, yeah! How you been?"

"Come on, Tommy. Enough of this. Let's eat."

Bud escorted the shivering hustler into the restaurant, where Tommy ordered his favorite meal -- steak medium and eggs over easy with hash browned potatoes, toast and hot, hot chocolate. "Same for me," Bud seconded. "But coffee for me and water for both of us."

Tommy stared blankly at the table, still shivering although trying to hide it.

"Where's your coat?"

"I... I traded it... for something to eat."

"When?"

"Couple of days ago."

"Hope you got two day's worth of eating for it."

The manner in which Tommy attacked his meal said otherwise.

The first time Bud ever saw Tommy Haynes was a hot July night in 1975. Tommy was in one of those truck aisles on hands and knees, blood dripping from busted lip and fist-extracted teeth. He helped the young man into Lisa, his pre-Matilda Peterbilt. Bud got Tommy inside and patched him up best he could with his first-aid kit and always-plentiful supply of paper towels taken from fuel stations.

"Here, let me wet this." Bud soaked a wad of towels with fresh coffee poured from his recently-filled thermos. He cleaned the blood from Tommy's face, tossed those towels and handed him dry ones. "Hold these on your gums." After the bleeding subsided a bit, Bud coerced him to talk. "What's your name?"

"Tommy."

"Who did this?"

"Guy I sucked off."

"What was he supposed to pay you?"

"Five bucks."

"Gave you a fist instead, huh?"

"Yeah... several. That stuff happens."

"Where's his truck?"

"It's red... got orange flames... said, uh... Burnin' Desire."

"You hungry?"

"Yeah."

"Come on. Let's eat."

Tommy ordered the same meal that first night, while Bud drank coffee. He gave their waitress the amount of the ticket plus ten dollars. "Charlotte," he read the name on her uniform. "Take care of my partner here until I get back."

Bud never told Tommy that he spent the next fifteen minutes finding the Burnin' Desire, knocking on its door and dragging its driver to the pavement. Never mind that the fellow was a good three inches taller and wider than Bud. Bud beat the man silly, focusing on the hideously oversized, soft belly hanging over his low, riding-at-the-crotch belt. He fist-pounded blubber to pulp. And when the man was allowed to collapse and lay on his side clutching his gut, Bud further unleashed his rage with his boot of choice -- brown, lace-up, Red Wing plain-toe hunting boots, his plain-toe stomping and kicking giving no regard to hands and arms covering the man's belly. Bud's victim opened his defense to save his limbs, surrendering to Bud's boot as it pulverized pulped belly muscle into jelly. And just as was done outside the trucker's tavern in Cheyenne, Bud said nothing, leaving it for the man to decide whether or not he should change his ways.

After catching his breath and straightening himself up, Bud returned to the restaurant, where Tommy sat with plate empty.

"Still hungry?"

"I got some ice cream and a piece of cake coming."

"I'll join you."

Bud sent Charlotte to duplicate Tommy's slice of chocolate for him, after she'd filled Bud's coffee mug. "You want more hot chocolate?"

"No."

Bud never asked Tommy why he had chosen his dangerous lifestyle. He never gave Tommy any money or accepted Tommy's blow job offer as a repayment. He took Tommy to the merchandise area of this truck stop and bought whatever items of clothing he desired, happy that Tommy chose basic needs of socks, underwear, jeans and shirts. Tommy took his new wardrobe into the men's rest room, leaving the old behind in the trash can before emerging with a simple, "Thank you, mister." And then, he returned to the trucker's aisles and went back to work.

Any stopover at this Salt Lake City truck stop would find Bud looking for Tommy, sometimes finding him and sometimes not, but each meeting would begin and end the same. Tommy never again fell prey to the fists of any man, not after Bud had given him a quick lesson in throwing a left jab, left hook, right cross combination. With this ammunition, Tommy protected himself.

Guessing at Tommy's shoe size, Bud kept a brand new pair of Red Wings in his tractor, presenting them on their next meeting, and little by little with each hook-up, Bud gave Tommy constructive suggestions on how to alter his career path.

Apparently, Bud's suggestions had gotten through on that January night when Bud last saw Tommy wearing the winter coat Bud had just purchased for him, Red Wings still on his feet with plenty of wear to go.

Bud was anxious for Tommy to fill in the gaps of his two-year absence, but for now he watched Tommy efficiently hook up the Freightliner to his towing unit, pull it out from underneath the trailer and maneuver it halfway off of the asphalt near the crash barrier, done with a four-point move forward and back, transmission scraping beneath but following. Bud was impressed. He watched Tommy disconnect and waved to him as he left the ramp. With Tommy and the Freightliner out of the way, Jack began his work with Bud standing off the ramp to give him plenty of space.

Jack pulled his Peterbilt in front, and then reversed under the semi-trailer and latched it onto his metal skid plate. Bolted atop the tractor's chassis, this horseshoe-shaped connector received the coupler mounted beneath the trailer. Once the trailer coupler slid into the hole of the plate, Jack got out of the cab and together he and Bud raised the legs of the trailer, hooked up the air hoses for braking and connected the electric wires to run the trailer lights.

"Now, look here. I hope you're not planning to judge my trailer-backing skills." Jack needled Bud as he climbed into the passenger's side of the Peterbilt.

"Jack Morton, all I wanna do is get some place where there's no traffic noise and I can relax with a cup of joe. Anything I can do to help you get me there, you let me know and I'll do it."

Bud leaned back in his seat so Jack could have an unobstructed view of the side mirror, and Jack talked while he worked. "Tell you what." The tractor and trailer inched backwards. "You put on one heck of a skid. Don't know how you kept from jack-knifing."

"Me neither. Situation like that, you don't think, you just do."

"How fast you reckon you were going when you hit the ramp?"

"Eighty-five thereabouts, last I looked."

"Man, oh, man. Lucky you're load didn't shift on that little turn."

"Must be packed in there tight." Bud answered each of Jack's comments without much thought, realizing that some drivers talk when they work whether anyone is there with them or not. It's a form of concentration. Bud frequently used this method himself, and so he knew he could respond to Jack's continuing statements with unrelated gibberish if he so desired, such as the just-begun baseball season or stories of his Navy days or the weather in Pocatello. It wouldn't have mattered because Jack would never have heard a word of it. Bud watched the side mirror while giving simple yes or no comebacks to Jack's ceaseless comments. With a steady backing of the trailer, Jack retraced Bud's path along the same skid marks of tire tread. One by one, metal parts of transmission and whatever else had broken apart emerged from the center of Jack's Peterbilt front bumper. Silently and with no movement, Bud said farewell to the Lincoln Highway. Six minutes later, Jack had the unit past the ramp entrance sign.

As they cleared the ramp, a car that had been waiting was allowed in by Paul Henderson.

"There's your insurance man," Jack pointed.

"I hope he appreciates the skills of a man who can back out a trailer without running over the evidence. Guess he'll be picking through the mess I made."

"Every inch." Jack stared at Bud, waiting for him to turn his head where a smile was waiting for him. Jack and Bud were members of an exclusive club. Both had seen what the other could do behind the wheel of a tractor-trailer and both were impressed. "Ready, Bud?"

"Yes, sir."

With Trooper Henderson following, warning lights flashing, Jack Morton finished Bud's slow ride down to the valley with an injured trailer wobbling in tow.

"Welcome to Salt Lake City, Bud Richter."

Maggie Pie

Down Time, Up Time

On the west side of Salt Lake, where I-80 briefly turns north to skirt the downtown skyscrapers, a street called California Avenue runs east and west south of the Union Pacific rail yards. Here is where most of the truck terminals also reside, such as the BXM Transport Leasing facility.

After opening its doors, Jack docked the rear of Bud's trailer to one of their loading bays, and then he waited for other BXM employees to lower the trailer legs before disconnecting. Parked nearby was Trooper Henderson's patrol car. He and Bud met midway between auto and Peterbilt.

"Looks like you're in good hands now."

"Paul, I want to thank you for everything. You don't know how good it was to see you coming down that ramp."

"Here. I wrote down these numbers." He pointed to the back of a Highway Patrol business card. "This is my home phone and this is my beeper number. Do you know how those work?"

"Yep. I punch the number I want you to call."

"Right. You call me anytime you're in this part of Utah. I live here and patrol the region east of here."

"Ok..." Bud was unsure as to why he was being given this information, until Paul's gaze of mutual understanding reminded him. The two men had something in common, details of which had yet to be learned. Paul's invitation to discuss them was personal, not professional. "I will do that, Paul. I certainly will."

Rejoining Jack, Bud rode with him in disconnecting from the trailer's coupler. They parked the Peterbilt amongst the rest of the terminal fleet of yard tractors, where nearby sat Tommy's towing unit idle and empty.

"Should I get my stuff out of the tow?"

"I suspect Tommy's got it. Let's look and see." Everything was right where Bud had left it on the passenger seat. "Hmm... Tommy's got this thing about not touching other people's property."

That's because Tommy had for so long suffered other people taking his meager belongings. Bud would have explained this to Jack had he been in the mood. With duffel and paperwork in hand, Bud took the short walk with Jack to the office.

"How long has BXM been in business, Jack?"

"Hmm... twelve years. This is my tenth. We'll break down your trailer and transfer to one of ours. Don't know the time. I suspect about two hours."

One long building housed eight loading docks and an office at the end, where one entry lane and one exit lane were separated by one shack occupied by one man who served as security guard and inspector for ingoing and outgoing traffic, same as the setup at the Pearsall terminal

Up four steps and the two men stood outside the office door. "Bud, let's go in here and Penny will take care of you. My shift's about over, so I doubt I'll be around when you pull out of here."

"Jack, I sure do appreciate you coming to my rescue. Your service is top-notch."

"Hey, you ain't too bad yourself. Believe me, I've seen some bad wrecks. Yours should have been."

A handshake preceded Jack's entry to the office with Bud in tow. "Penny, this is Bud Richter from Pearsall Truck Lines. You be nice to him. He's had one hell of a bad day."

"So, I've heard. Come with me, you poor thing. I'll get whatever you need."

The first thing he needed was to urinate. Penny showed him where to do that. Next she took him to the owner's office, where a comfy leather couch sat waiting. "Mr. Barlow's gone for the day, but said for you to rest here. Are you hungry?"

Bud's watch showed nearly five p.m. "I guess I should be, but I'd rather have some coffee first."

With his request granted, Bud listened to Penny explain details. "Your load has been rescheduled for delivery at noon Sacramento time. I have all your new paperwork here. Give me the old."

He did and she removed the contents of his packet, offering Bud the chance to inspect her new papers before stuffing them inside. He declined.

"Now," she continued. "Your new trailer will be ready by eight o'clock tonight. When would you like to leave our terminal?"

The running of his fingers through his hair failed to stimulate Bud's weary brain to work. "Ah... let's see... I gotta eat... probably should try to sleep... I can't even think how far..."

"Sacramento is five hundred thirty-three miles. Estimated driving time eight hours with no stops, so I suggest you leave by three a.m. You will gain one hour crossing into Pacific Time Zone."

Bud stared blankly with packet on lap, still unable to make logical decisions. The comfort of leather couch beneath him unraveled the trauma of his mishap, the built-up tension released all at once to cloud his judgement. He fought to delay what Trooper Henderson knew would come, and did so by focusing on the woman assigned to help him. Her grey business suit remained crisp despite the approaching end of her work day. It's tailored lines defined a shapely female trim, fit and fresh. He imagined her moving to lock the door. Rejoining him, she unbuttons the top three of his shirt, telling him to relax, unwind. She sympathizes with the suffering he has endured, tells him that he is quite a man to have survived such an ordeal. It is the least she can do for him, helping him to relieve his pressure, as she unbuckles his belt, unsnaps his jeans and lowers his zipper. She exposes his penis, folding back his underwear to reveal its swollen readiness. She leaves her red lipstick smeared to his shaft, as she gently squeezes him between her tongue and roof of mouth. She...

"Mr. Richter."

"Huh?" Bud opens his eyes.

"Tommy Haynes has volunteered to take care of you during your stay with us. He will take you to his home, where you can eat, sleep and shower, if you wish."

"Tommy Haynes?"

"Our tow truck driver. Remember?"

"Oh, sure... uh, yeah. That should work. Um..." Bud knew his peter was erect. He was more than relieved to see his new paperwork packet conveniently hiding the fact from her. "Let's schedule my departure for two a.m." Bud's quick fantasy had stirred his brain to function. "What tractor will I be driving?"

"We use Peterbilt road tractors with sleepers."

"Perfect. Two a.m. I'll be ready to go."

"We will have you ready to go." She handed him an ink pen and clipboard. Your Mr. Jacobs would like for you to fill out this report. I will call him in the morning and read the information over the phone. Do you need to make any phone calls?"

"No, ma'am. Not right now."

"You work on this. I'll get Tommy."

With a bit of grumbling, Bud sat alone with clipboard, wondering why Mr. Jacobs couldn't get the same damned information from the Utah Highway Patrol. When Tommy entered, their reunion started with a hug and much enthusiasm, toned down a bit with the arrival of Penny.

"Mr. Richter, I'm turning you over to Tommy. My day is finished. It was a pleasure to meet you."

Bud stood, confident of his flaccid state, and verbally thanked this kind woman for her professional assistance, while silently thanking her for his dreamed moment of orgasm.

Tommy's residence was about twenty minutes away, an apartment towards downtown, near I-80 and not too far from the B & D Truck Stop Restaurant where they used to meet.

"So, how'd you do it, Tommy?" Bud asked while riding in Tommy's auto.

"Just like you told me. I applied at every dock around here. Got hired on a probationary basis loading and breaking down trailers."

"How long ago?"

"A year ago January. Jack liked my work and started showing me how to drive the hostler tractors."

"How'd you get into the towing part of it?"

"Guy showed up drunk. They fired him and Jack suggested I train for the job. Been doing that four months now."

"Like the job?"

"Are you kidding? Teamster's Union, full benefits, even got my teeth fixed. Look." He turned towards Bud with a grimacing grin. "They're custom-made, screwed onto my bones like I was born with 'em."

"My, my... ain't you handsome?"

"You ain't seen nothing yet."

Tommy escorted Bud into his second-floor, two-bedroom apartment. "Bud Richter, this is my wife, Jackie... and my daughter, Brenda."

A handsome, blond-haired woman held an infant wrapped in cuddly blanket. "Hello, Bud. Tommy called to tell me he'd finally found you. Here, Tommy, take her." Free of her child, Jackie embraced their guest. "Welcome to our home." She kissed Bud's cheek. "And that means anytime you want."

Bud had no problem fawning over Tommy's three-month-old baby girl, nor did he hesitate to down Jackie's version of steak and eggs, ordered by her husband for nostalgia's sake. Conversation was focused on the present, not the past, as Bud shared wallet pictures of his children, and unlike previous opportunities, this time Tommy showed great interest in the Richter kids, forcing Bud to detail their lives for him.

Hours could have been spent telling tales, had Bud not been exhausted. He was given the Haynes's bedroom.

"No couch for you," Tommy explained to Bud's protest. "You get a soft bed with clean sheets. I'll wake you up at twelve-thirty, you can shower, grab a bite and I'll have you at our terminal by two."

"What would you like for road food, Bud?" Jackie asked.

"Jackie, a big bowl of oatmeal stays with me for hours. If you've got any."

"We will have plenty."

By seven-thirty p.m., Bud was stripped to his undershorts and snugly nestled beneath sheet and blanket. Tommy was there, removing something from his closet.

"Lookee here." He held up the Red Wings. "Still got your boots. Still wear 'em, too."

"Good deal, Tommy. They'll last forever if you take care of 'em like I told you."

"I do." He sat on the edge of the mattress. "Everything you told me came true." He placed the palm of his hand onto Bud's blanket-covered chest. "Wish I'd have listened to you the first time I saw you." He lowered his lips to Bud's forehead, leaving behind a gentle kiss. "I owe you everything."

"No you don't, Tommy. You've repaid me... got your shit together. That's all I ever wanted from you."

Another kiss was accompanied with moisture smeared from cheek to forehead, a tear of good riddance to the old Tommy, a tear of gratitude for the man who enabled the new Tommy. "I love you, Bud. Sleep well."

Bad Cargo

Bud's brain was a fine-tuned machine when it came to sleeping. He could turn it off or on whenever he desired, regardless of caffeine, regardless of the hour of day or number of hours between, regardless of whatever events had occurred during those hours between. Occasionally, once Bud got to sleep no one else could sleep near him, what with his snoring and sporadic bad dreams, but that was their problem, not his.

Since neither Jackie nor Tommy nor Brenda liked oatmeal, Tommy went out to buy some so that a hot bowl was ready to eat after Bud had showered and dressed. Tommy dropped him at the terminal at 01:45:00 with phone numbers exchanged and promises to stay in contact.

The night-time terminal manager greeted Bud and pointed to his unit, Peterbilt engine rumbling and fresh semi-trailer hooked and ready.

"When you leave here turn right," the manager pointed to hand-held map. "You'll catch I-80 after it's turned west out of downtown. Saves you about thirty minutes." He gave the city map to Bud.

"Appreciate it." Bud was escorted inside, where he called Pearsall to report his departure time, filled his thermos with coffee, and pissed. At 01:58:00 Bud climbed into the cab of his Peterbilt and executed the same routine as always. Walk-around done, trailer doors shut and secured, he removed the log book from his seat-resting duffel, organized his paperwork, and familiarized himself with his surroundings. Little time was needed for this 1976 model of tractor. His pre-Matilda tractor had been a 1973 model named Lisa. He instantly named this red BXM version Lisa Two.

"Oh, my god! You beautiful thing, you," was Bud's reaction to an item he saw in the dash -- an eight-track tape deck. He immediately dug into the bottom of his duffel and extracted every cartridge he could feel. "Oh, yeah, baby. You're first... make sure this thing works." The beautiful baritone of Jim Reeves permeated the cab. "We've got action." Bud shifted into gear, eased out of the terminal and sang along, changing a word or two to make the song fit his mood. *Put your sweet lips a little closer to the bone. And tell your friend, I don't do three-ways, he'll have to go.*

Entering I-80 near the airport, Bud quickly was in darkness. "Damdest place I've ever seen. One minute you're in the city and the next nothing." Bud made this observation every time he headed west out of Salt Lake, but this time with less conviction. He thought of the good folks at BXM, and of Trooper Paul, and of Tommy, Jackie and baby Brenda, comforted to know that he had good reasons to like Utah, or at least some of the people living there.

What lay ahead was one hundred miles of flat and straight, keyword flat, as in Salt Flats. Mile after mile of nothing but white. Ribbons of highway as far as the eye can see. So monotonous and unobstructed that you can actually see the curvature of the planet earth, but not at night. Bud drove in silence, entertaining any thought that came into his head. Despite the availability of his self-recorded compilation of favorite songs on tape, he for now preferred the constant hum of engine, listening intently to confirm its flawless performance. After what the Freightliner had put him through, the sounds of efficiency were the only sounds he desired.

In his duffel was a one-pound bag of peanut M & M's, Harry's favorite, the perfect way to keep a stomach happy when no stops were planned for many a mile. Two at a time did the trick, a slow melt of candy shell and chocolate, no teeth involved until down to the peanut. A sip of coffee washed it down, preparing the mouth for its next insertion.

His brain did replay the harrowing, downhill ride towards Salt Lake, but rather than concocting scenarios of disaster, his thoughts centered on Julie, Lisa and Jack, mostly Lisa and Jack. Here is where the questions of doubt played their tricks with him, which coerced Bud into a solitary conversation with himself:

What if they'd lost me? Who would support them? Have I done all I can do? Ah, hell. Give them what they need and leave 'em alone, that's what I say. Kids oughtta be able to do whatever they want. Childhood should be fun, because lord knows being a grownup is a pain in the ass by comparison. Why stress them with strict rules for no good reason? Money's no problem. Whatever Lisa and Jack need or want, I'll buy it. But maybe I should somehow prepare them for adulthood, too. Shit, they never ask me anything like that. Maybe they're afraid to. Maybe I oughtta take the initiative on that part of it.

"Oh, fuck this," Bud ended it. "Drive myself nuts with this crap." He pushed in the tape to hear Tammy Wynette singing *Good lovin' keeps a home together...* "It sure does, Tammy, but from a distance."

By Bud's way of thinking, his divorce agreement with Julie was the greatest gift he could ever have bestowed upon Lisa and Jack. He gave their mother the house, while he kept the land surrounding it. This guaranteed that his kids would always have a roof over their heads, for it was also written that the house could never be sold unless both parties agreed. Considering the pre-separation rows that Lisa and Jack had to endure on a nightly basis, Bud was amazed at how he and their mother had created a stable environment for them in recent years after Julie had discovered within one year of marriage that Charlie Hofstra was nothing more than a freeloader; after Bud had removed himself from the Richter farm, the place where long before he'd even met Julie the seeds of his pain were planted.

"Ah, fuck it, man. Cut this shit out." Bud quickly jumped off that train of thought before it could take him to unfriendly places.

The lights of Wendover, the first seen in eighty miles of travel, shined as the portal to Nevada, and ten miles later he was there. It was four a.m. He adjusted his watch to Pacific time, making it three a.m. Bud hoped to cross the state and hit Reno by seven. There was nothing to stop him but himself -- no traffic, very few exits, and little to see even if there had been daylight.

A billboard in Wendover advertising a fight in Las Vegas brought Bud a chuckle. "Larry Holmes versus Leroy Jones? That was last month. Time to take that one down. Eighth round knockout, kinda like the night I ran Charlie out of town."

"Charlie was too stupid for his own good. Hell, I didn't mind him living there. As long as he just sat on his ass, drank his beer and watched television, didn't try to play daddy with my kids, I couldn't have cared less. It's when he started bringing that god damned Harold Turley over... and Ronnie Stover... that was a major fuck-up on his part. He should have done a little history about me and Turley. Pissed me off that Julie never said anything to me. Thank god Maggie did. I got 'em. Got 'em good. I knew they'd show up at Joe's Tavern. Never dreamed they'd bring Charlie with 'em, though. That was rich. Knocked the shit outta all three of 'em. Nothing like a left hook to the liver. That'll put a man down every time. Ain't that right, Larry Holmes... Ha, ha... they got the message. Damned hayseeds. Ha... Julie never even tried to stop ol' Charlie from going back to Bum Fuck, Kansas... or wherever the hell he came from. Didn't take her long to file for divorce, did it? Solved that little issue real quick. Turley's never said a word to me since... never will, either. Bastard.

Dim lights, thick smoke, and loud, loud music. The timing of that one couldn't have been better. Reno was in view. Bud had effectively whiled away the hours and miles, arriving on the other side of the state with the rising sun reflecting in his side-view mirrors and the dimming lights of distant Reno in his windshield.

His butt hurt, his legs were stiff, the arches of his feet cramped, so he exited into the final Nevada-maintained rest area to stretch, empty his piss bottle and evacuate in a real, working urinal. Then, he drove. The load behind him was bad cargo. Those screws and bolts had participated in his first-ever accident, and he wanted rid of them. Bud wanted that cargo dropped where it belonged as soon as possible.

Crossing into California would make him forget his quickly-returning aches and pains. Bud was about to get a workout, as was his equipment. The Sierra Nevada Mountains climb along the Trukee River, heading for Donner Pass where I-80 reaches seventy-two hundred feet. Then begins a steady descent complete with fifty-mile-per-hour curves to negotiate as well, all at a five-degree grade. For the next forty miles, Buds arms, legs, eyes, hands and feet would be very busy indeed. When finished, Bud's descent to the town of Alta lowered him to thirty-six hundred feet, and although the concrete continued to grade down a few more hundred, the final sixty miles to Sacramento was smooth sailing by comparison.

Bud took a deep breath, arched back his toes to relieve the foot cramps, and finished the last of his carefully rationed coffee. With straight highway ahead, he spread open his map and confirmed his planned route to the Sacramento delivery point. "Zimmerman Hardware Supply, Sutterville Road. Hell, I know exactly where that is. Off the Five by the river. Been there before. Bastards better have an open bay for me to dump this."

They did. Bud was two hours early, so he parked the rig in an open area beyond the docks and put his feet onto concrete. He stretched. He yawned. He climbed into the cab to grab his paperwork, taking it into the Zimmerman warehouse office for permission to drop his trailer. Granted, bay two. He backed into the hole, lowered the trailer legs, unhooked air and electrical hoses, dropped his trailer and headed for the nearest truck stop known to him, off of Interstate Five southbound. Gone, out of business, so he kept going.

Fatigue was quickly taking over. With his burdensome load finally delivered, nothing scheduled, no assignments, Bud's adrenal glands had no reason to keep him going. But his stomach had good reason. The only question was *if* he could soon find a truck stop and *if* it had a full-service restaurant, could he stay awake long enough to find a seat, order anything that sounded good and wait for it to arrive.

Six miles later, a billboard advertised Hank's Truck Plaza, three miles ahead on the right. He made it, found an open spot in the trucker's aisle, parked and shut down the Peterbilt -- good old Peterbilt.

"Jenny, this is Bud checking in." He sat alone in a four-person booth. The table butted the wall beneath a window to his left overlooking fuel pumps reserved for automobiles. Attached to the same wall was a telephone, as with every wall table, installed for the convenience of truck drivers. He'd ordered steak, eggs, coffee and water before calling his Pearsall office collect.

"Bud? Are you all right?"

"Yes."

"Why didn't you call me? I've been worried to death."

"I figured Jacobs had told you."

"He did, but I expected to hear from you. Damn it, Bud. I needed to hear from you."

"Hold on, my coffee's here." His coffee wasn't there, not yet. Bud needed a minute to compose himself. His mental state made him vulnerable to an explosive response to conflict of any sort, and a scolding from some woman who cared more about him at that moment than he did her definitely qualified as crap he didn't need. With a deep breath and fingers rubbing his forehead, he answered. "Jenny, I'm sorry, but after what happened I just wanted to get this delivery over with. I didn't think. I just drove straight through from Salt Lake to Sacramento and I'm a little tired right now."

Playing the sympathy angle calmed Jenny a bit. "Ok, Bud. You know I worry about you, that's all."

"Well, there's no need. Worry will put you in an early grave, darling. Stop it." He covered the mouthpiece and thanked the waitress, who sat a tall glass of ice water and cup of coffee in front of him. "Ok, Jenny, Unit B1247, or whatever you called it after the trailer switch... it was dropped at ten a.m. to Zimmerman's. I'm at Hank's Truck Plaza on Interstate Five about ten miles south of Sacramento. Don't know what exit I took. I will check in again at five p.m. Pacific time. Ok?"

"Yes, Bud. I got it. Get some rest."

"That's the plan."

"Goodbye, Bud... You know I... goodbye, Bud."

That was close to being uncomfortable. Those three words spoken by Tommy touched Bud deeply, but the same words from a woman already married to another man could be nothing but trouble. Females scattered across the entire country eagerly accepted Bud's call, always ready for his expertly delivered poke. Chosen by him for their commitment to non-committal, they made the most of his time and never protested when their time with him was up. Jenny was different. Jenny could become serious if she ever freed herself from her husband, a prospect which Bud refused to consider unless it happened. Until it did, if it ever did, then he would be forced to figure out what to do about it. As things were, he saw no need to probe his emotions on the subject of Jenny.

Bud had no female connections anywhere near Sacramento, not that he would have called one in his present state. After filling his belly, he headed towards his tractor, where a sleeping bunk awaited. Showering would have to wait.

As he cleared the corner of the restaurant, a scratchy voice called out. "Hey, mishter. Got time to play?"

Still walking, Bud turned his head. It was a trucker's hag, probably thirty but looked fifty. "How much for a BJ?"

"Ten."

"And a screw?"

"Twenty."

"I'll take the BJ. Come on."

She followed him to the door of his bunk. He unlocked and opened it. "Here's ten. Step on up."

With black high-heeled pumps scuffed and scraped to grey, she placed one foot on the first step, raised herself and failed to connect the heel of her second foot to the surface. She fell backwards into Bud's arms.

"Are you drunk?"

"No, no, no... ha... I'm ok, mishter."

"No you ain't. Get on out of here. Keep the money."

"Aw, come on, shweetie," she turned to face him, eyes glazed, mascara messy. "I'll be good to ya."

"Nope. No drunk's gonna slobber on me. Take your money and move on, now, before I turn you in."

"Aw, please mishter," she took hold of his arm and pulled herself close to him. "I don't care about the money. I need a man."

"There's hundreds of 'em around here. Now, go on. Get away from me." Bud thrust his arm forward to cast off her grip. She stumbled, not from the force of Bud's arm, but from the clumsiness of her tipsy state, tumbling with a meaty thud of her buttocks to hard asphalt.

"Damn, woman." Bud offered his hand to help her to her feet. "Are you ok?"

"Get away from me, you son of a bish."

He stood by while she rolled to her knees, stood, hand brushed her hopelessly messed hair, and staggered towards the restaurant.

"Lucked out there," Bud mumbled to himself. "What the hell was I thinking?"

Forces working against Bud had coerced him into a bad decision, one that he seldom made. Fatigue made him vulnerable. Discomfort with Jenny's over-abundance of concern caused him to accept the solicitation of nasty mouth for hire, but his protectors, as Trooper Paul Henderson called them, had kindly intervened. And the memory of Paul's comforting gaze calmed Bud as he climbed up into his bunk, closing and locking the door behind him.

Bud took off his shirt, removed his boots and opened up his jeans. He solved his growing problem all by himself with the combined effort of his right hand and another memory. He completed his fantasy of pretty Penny, the BXM secretary in Salt Lake who was too professional to give Bud anything more than the essentials needed to deliver his load -- the load in his trailer, not his nuts. Unfortunately, Bud had forgotten to stock his leased tractor with paper towels. A dirty white sock from yesterday taken from his duffel absorbed the wasted seed from his belly, and Bud instantly fell into a contented sleep with jeans open, peter exposed, and sticky sock clutched in his right hand.

Whirlwind

Refreshed, Bud put in his request for a shower stall, finding the facilities at Hank's poorly-kept, which justified his reason for always wearing shower sandals. But water and soap never fail to invigorate a man. With fresh clothes, energy and attitude, Bud again sat in restaurant booth calling the Pearsall office. Jenny had planned a productive tour for his return trip, but she had left for the day so it was Martina who told him the details.

After topping off first his stomach and then his tractor's one-hundred-gallon fuel tank, he bobtailed south on I-5 to Bakersfield, picked up a trailer to pull east on State Highway 58 to Barstow. There, he waited, sleeping in his sleeper until the warehouse opened its doors at six a.m. After dropping that one he found a place for breakfast, got another load and traveled I-40 out of California into Arizona -- destination Flagstaff, along what was U.S. Route 66 skirting the southern edge of the Grand Canyon. More ghosts. Good ghosts, because after dropping his load in Flagstaff, Bud was granted several hours of freedom to call his favorite Flagstaff female, Wanda.

"Hey, pretty lady, Bud Richter."

"Hi, Bud. Where are you?"

"Flying Homo Motel."

"Oh, Bud. You are too funny."

"Can you do me?"

"It'll be a couple hours before I can get away."

"Room Sixteen."

"Ok, hot thing. Wait for me."

"I will wait for you until hell freezes... or until I get a better offer."

Wanda was there in one hour and a half. Adjacent to the Flying F truck plaza the Flying F Motel provided comfortably clean beds for sleeping and other activities. Wanda was ready for the second choice, as she knocked on door Sixteen.

"There she is. My Arizona beauty queen."

"Oh, honey, you should have seen me back in the day."

"I like you on this day. Get your ass in here."

He swatted that ass when she stepped past him. Shirtless, sockless, with jeans and sandals his only attire, Bud peeled back the bed coverings from a double-sized mattress and stripped himself down to nothing. "I got coffee."

"Don't need it." Wanda sat her purse onto the dresser and used the area of a table and chair combination to strip herself naked. "Where you been? You little ape man."

"You call this little?" Bud stood with hands on hips, his penis swollen and decidedly separated from his balls.

"A little too long since I've seen it. Too bad your company doesn't send you around here more often."

"All hell, they don't want us to get bored. Besides, you'd get tired of me."

"That'll never happen." She sprawled on her back with arms uplifted to accept him, as Bud crushed her breasts beneath his furry chest. "Come on in, Bud. I've been needing you."

Communication was limited to the physical, with the exception of Wanda's verbal expressions of pleasure directed towards him to further excite herself. Bud's philosophy was to beat the pussy to death, not in a cruel way, but with powerful, masculine domination like a Trojan warrior, targeting her clitoris while filling its surroundings with angled thrusts from every direction. His penetration was never deep. His assault emphasized his mass, his swollen corona efficiently distributing its strength to her where she needed it most -- the top of her zipper, her center of entry and her encapsulating meat three inches within.

Bud brought her no pain, only joy, and Wanda clutched her fingertips into his muscle-writhing back, scraping his tiny hairs with her thumbs. She clenched the muscles between her legs as though defending her G-spot from his attack, which intensified the effectiveness of his attack. Her hands pressed him to her breasts, raising the temperature of heated friction, his hard pectorals, his soft chest hairs rubbing her nipples. She expressed her pleasure with each all-consuming, inward thrust of his powerful tool. "Oh... Bud... you... beautiful... man... you... strong... ass... gorilla... you... fucking... Neanderthal... you... "

Her words transformed to high-pitched moans, music to Bud's ears. He waited for her, saving his voice and his bounty for her completion. And as her vibrating innards signaled the height of her pleasure, Bud expressed himself in a deep-throated and graveled growl, fitting for a Neanderthal, fitting for a male animal, unleashing his milk to mesh with hers.

She clamped both hands to his muscular butt cheeks, forcing him to remain with her, forcing him to deep penetration. This is where she wanted him to be. His full weight bearing down on her, his head nestled in the crook of her shoulder, she lovingly massaged his back, nibbled his ear, while relishing the slow fade of his penis inside her. Its still-powerful thickness scraped her vaginal walls in a retreat of micro-inches, and she treasured each increment of remaining ecstasy, hoping he would never leave.

Bud did leave, but only because his penis slipped out from shrinkage. He rolled onto his back with arms sprawled, his breathing rapid but controlled. Wanda moved onto her side and rested her head on his right pectoral, her right hand gently rubbing his belly. As he wrapped his right arm across her back, his rough hand on her soft shoulder, Wanda kissed Bud's nipple, whispered that she could eat him alive. He never responded. His nasal passages relaxed to cause a faint snoring. "Such a man," she thought, and she proceeded to eat him alive.

With a snoozing man sprawled naked before her, Wanda lathered his body with kisses wet and dry from his chest to his toes. She climaxed her feast with her chest laying between his thighs. She kissed his nuts, licked them, pinched their skin with her delicate lips, and then tasted her own juice on his slumbering penis. It swelled for her, but not to full strength. His second orgasm was not her intent. Wanda was hungry, hungry for a man, and her insatiable appetite consumed this man as he contentedly lay surrendered for the taking.

Time of Day

A one-hour nap culminated with Bud dropping his secondary load into Wanda's belly.

"Mmm, that was nice. Thank you, darlin'."

"Got time to do me?"

"Don't know. Got a trailer pick-up in about an hour... heading for Albuquerque... probably ought to... " Bud was hungry, too. "Ah, what the hell. Spread it on out there, momma."

Bud's oral expertise was second only to his penile, and he had Wanda howling within fifteen minutes.

"Oh, Bud, nobody party's like you. When are you coming back?"

"Never know."

"Will you call me?"

"You know I will."

"Am I first on your list?"

"Are you kidding. Best BJ and screw combination in the southwest. Who else would I call?"

"You better. These young drivers got no class. No appreciation for what experience can give 'em. Don't know what I'll do when the likes of you are dead and gone."

"Well, sweetheart, you'll be dead and gone with us. We'll do it there. Ok?"

"Kiss me goodbye."

After receiving a quick smooch and another butt-swat out the door, Wanda returned Bud to the realities of the road. Mid-morning in Albuquerque he dropped, waited two hours with a meal and a fuel tank fill-up, and then grabbed the trailer that would follow him home. A 45-footer, filled with boxed textiles. He'd bring it to the Pearsall terminal and leave it for them to do with as they pleased.

Northbound on I-25, Bud knocked out the cities along his four-hundred-thirty-mile trip one by one. Santa Fe, New Mexico to Colorado Springs, Colorado, done. What day was it? He didn't know. He'd need to check his log book. Day or night? It didn't matter. Road drivers exist from pick-up to delivery, not by days or hours. When their body says go, they go, until their body says stop to eat, stop to sleep. In between, when they work, they entertain themselves with music, with chatter on the CB radio, with sights and sounds of the road, with sights and sounds of the countryside that weren't there the previous time they'd come through.

Bud's stomach told him to stop in Pueblo, Colorado. A dated, bedraggled, Native American owned truck plaza was within walking distance to Marcie's Restaurant, one of his favorite eating joints of any encountered on his long list.

"Best ten dollar steak in the entire country," he told his waitress. She was too young to perceive Bud's comment as anything more than a come-on, but he made sure she knew he was one hundred percent sincere. "Tell the cook I said so, and I've eaten in a thousand restaurants. I know what I'm talking about." He chuckled at her smirk, doubting that she would tell the cook anything other than she had another smart-ass to deal with. Bud overlooked her bad attitude in anticipation of his favorite meal.

He used a payphone to check in collect with Pearsall. Gave his location and estimated time of arrival to Jenny. Thanked her for setting up his return trip so perfectly. Told her he'd be glad to see her, hoping that would put her mind at ease that she was on his list of very important people.

Resuming his northbound trek on I-25, Bud's brain still buzzed with memories of Wanda and all those like her in the many cities he had visited through his years of travel. Good women, fun women who enjoy the thrills of sex with no commitments, who never took any more from him than the pleasure of his company, which made them pleasurable to him. They didn't care if he called them at two in the afternoon or two in the morning. They didn't care if he was available for one hour or ten. Most important of all, they didn't care what or who he did after leaving their town. Bud had carefully cultivated his list of contacts, a list constantly changing. Some had married and some had disappeared, but he always managed to find replacements scattered throughout the country to relieve his stress.

Approaching Denver, Bud was a man driven with purpose. He could smell home. Some of the most beautiful scenery on the North American Continent, the Rocky Mountains, peaked in the distance to his left, but they were oblivious to him. He'd seen them countless times, many times driven right through them, but all he could see now was his simple apartment with its simple bed. His bed, broken in by him to fit his body, and Bud couldn't get there soon enough. Negotiating traffic through a major metropolitan area was the final challenge facing Bud, and once that was conquered and Fort Collins came and went with the front range of the Rocky Mountains nearby, the Wyoming state line seemed to surprise him with its quick arrival. Cheyenne was ten miles away, his Pearsall terminal, twenty.

Just before midnight, the end of Saturday and beginning of Sunday,

Bud turned onto the entry lane and stopped for check-in. There was Wally, chubby Wally. He stepped out of his Pearsall inspection shed and climbed up onto Bud's running board with clipboard in hand.

"Couldn't you wait 'til my shift was over? Ten minutes?"

"Well, here, I'll back out and come in later."

"Hey! This tractor's the wrong color."

"Yeah, but unlike Pearsall crap, this one has a transmission that works."

"Good to see you, Bud. Sounds like you had a rough one."

"One I won't forget."

Wally stepped down and Bud joined him on the ground, raising his arms above his head to stretch with back arched.

"Guess what, Bud?"

"What?" He followed Wally as they did a walk-around inspection of the rig.

"Same thing happened to Harry."

"What happened to Harry?"

"Company bought two new Freightliners. Harry took the other one east. Same thing. Gear box wouldn't take a gear."

"Where was he?"

"Outside Des Moines. Nice and flat, luckily."

"That's a hell of a thing. Was he coming or going."

"Coming back."

"They bring Harry back here?"

"Not yet. Harry's still in Des Moines, I guess. So's the tractor. Yours is still in Salt Lake."

"We'll probably be hearing about a recall on that model."

"Something's gonna happen." With his inspection complete, Wally raised the gate. "Park it in G-11, Bud. Leave it hooked up."

"Make me walk from the god damned lot. Thanks a lot, Wally."

"Just following orders."

"I know. See ya."

Bud liked Wally when Wally was sober. When he wasn't, he wallowed in self pity, which is hard to hear after an hour of it. Wally would have been the senior driver by now, had he not let his penchant for alcohol give him an added reason to feel sorry for himself. He messed up in Illinois. Fortunately, he damaged only Pearsall equipment and himself, not other vehicles nor the people inside, and had it not been for his prior twenty-three years of road sobriety, clean driving record and impeccable service to the company, Perry Jacobs would have terminated Wally's employment. Instead, Perry assigned him to sit in the guard house. It was his final chance to keep his pension, and so far, for two years, Wally had not abused his lucky break.

Bud took his time rolling to aisle G, paused three minutes before backing into slot 11 and did so with extra care. This is the time when a driver is most vulnerable to mishaps. After having been at it for six days, he's giddy to be back on his home terminal. He's hyper, tired and anxious to be done with it, which opens the door to stupid mistakes, to overlooking a procedure that normally would be automatic. Bud did not appreciate Wally's expecting him to back his rig into this slot. A hostler should have been assigned to do it later, so Bud could just park it and leave it safely home, his job done.

As Bud sat in the tractor closing out his log book, an act of kindness by Wally's replacement made Bud forget about Wally's gaffe. Pulling in front of Bud's rig, driving a former U.S. Postal Jeep purchased at auction by Pearsall to cart employees around their five-acre lot, the man shouted from open window.

"Wally sent me to get you."

"What?" Bud shouted back, coercing the man to exit the Jeep and approach the driver's side of Bud's tractor.

"Wally said to give you a ride back."

"Get in."

Circling in between the Jeep and front of the tractor, he stepped up onto the passenger-side running board and pressed the handle before realizing that his body was in the way. He shuffled to his left and swung open the door, reaching to move Bud's duffel so he could sit, but then hesitated.

"Oh, sorry. Let me throw that in the back." With the seat clear, Bud patted it with his hand. "There you go. Hey, I don't know you."

"Just started this week. I'm Robert Carlyle." He offered his hand, still standing on the running board.

Freeing his right hand of his writing pen, Bud leaned to the right and took that hand. "Bud Richter." He gently pulled him closer. "Come on in, Robert. Take a seat."

Bud estimated Robert to be in his early twenties, slender, a bit fragile and completely uncomfortable negotiating his entry to a tractor. Pretending not to notice, Bud resumed updating and closing out his log. "I appreciate you coming to get me, Robert. Just doing a little paperwork here. Making sure everything's in order, if you don't mind waiting."

"Oh, I better turn off the Jeep."

He started to bolt from the Peterbilt, but Bud stopped him. "It's ok, Robert. Sit down and relax. This company can afford a bit of gasoline."

"Not because I did it. I'll be right back." He opened the door and looked down, trying to decide whether to use the running board or jump to the pavement. Robert awkwardly stepped right foot onto the board, causing him to face the wrong direction when his left foot hit the lot. Bud smiled as Robert turned around and headed for the Jeep. Upon returning, Robert's second entry to the tractor was a bit less clumsy than the first, but only because Robert, perhaps on purpose but probably by dumb luck, had left the door open. Robert sat quietly, eyes straight ahead, hands clamped tightly to his thighs.

"So, how do you like it so far?" Bud kept writing, looking down to his log in a cab illuminated by overhead interior lights.

"So far, so good."

Quickly vague, thought Bud. "What I'm doing here is called unwinding. Letting my brain know it doesn't have to keep track of every little detail any more. Soon as my log book is closed out, my road trip is over, Robert, so let's just sit tight for awhile. Ok?"

"Ok."

"What did you do before coming here?"

"Nothing much."

"Another truck line?"

"No. Retail mostly. Convenience stores and stuff."

"That's a far cry from this line of work." Bud set aside his completed log book and looked at his passenger. "Do you like being around all these smelly trucks?"

Robert finally turned to his left. "Mr. Richter..."

"Bud."

"Bud, I love it here. Even when nothing's going on, it's exciting."

"Ever been in one of these?"

"No. You're the first one who's let me. In fact, you're the first driver who's spoken to me other than yes and no answers to questions I gotta ask."

"What do you think? Pretty strong stuff, huh?"

"Like your own little world. It's cool as hell."

"Yeah, being in here is a powerful thing." Bud put a friendly slap of his hand to the young man's knee cap. "Robert, you pay no mind to those drivers. Sure, some of 'em are ass holes and that's just the way it is. But most of 'em coming in are gonna be dead tired. Most of 'em going out got a million things running through their minds, thinking about the job they gotta do. So, don't take it personal. Once they get to know you, they'll loosen up a little bit."

"I understand. I can't be thin-skinned around here."

"That's a good way to put it. If they give you shit, just give it right back to 'em. Nine times out of ten, a man will respect you more when you stand up to him."

"Thanks, Bud." And to prove to Bud he planned to take his advice, Robert mimicked Bud by slapping Bud on his knee.

"Planning to drive one of these someday?"

"Ha... don't know if I ever could. I'd like to."

"No big deal. Just like a car, except it's ten times bigger... and stronger... and heavier. Get out and come around here."

When Robert reached the driver's side, Bud was standing on concrete waiting for him. "First thing you gotta do is learn how to get in the damn thing. Do it from the ground. Reach up there and swing that door open like you mean business."

Robert did as told, with conviction.

"Now, grab that handle, flex that bicep and step on up." He put his right foot on the running board. "No, son, other foot first." Robert started again with his left foot. "Swing your right foot in front of the left and get it on the floorboard. There you go, now sit your ass down."

He sat with hands on thighs, scanning lit gauges and switches, absorbing everything like a kid on Christmas morning. Losing all inhibitions, Robert put both hands onto the steering wheel, gripping it, and then sliding his palms over the entire surface. His right hand moved to the gear shifter, squeezed its hard, palm-filling roundness, felt the power of the engine vibrating from under the hood, through the gear shifter and all the way up into his forearm.

Bud stepped onto the running board, spreading his arms with one grip on the vertical handle bar and the other atop the open door. "Ok, Robert. This beautiful machine here just took me fifteen hundred miles, safely and with no complaints. It's time to shut her down, but we do it with respect and tender loving care. That's how we show her our appreciation for bringing us home in one piece."

Robert, grinning and eager, looked to Bud. "Where do we start?"

"Trailer lights. One for the frame. Right there." It was done. "Running lights, right there." The Peterbilt tractor's exterior went dark. "All the rest, right there." Tractor head and parking lights out; trailer tail out. "Right foot on the brake, left on the clutch. Go ahead, take it to the floor. Now, shifter to the left... more... now bring it down towards you... keep the clutch down... just like a car, turn the key."

Everything went silent, except for Robert's rapidly excited breathing.

"Clutch out... foot off the brake... and you're done."

84

"What about the parking brake?"

"Glad you asked. Been engaged ever since you pulled up. It's right there."

"Thanks, Bud."

"You're welcome, Robert. Hand me my bag... and my log book... and that big envelope. Come on, show me how to drive a Jeep."

As Bud opened the Jeep door, Robert yelled to him. "Hey Bud, light's on inside."

"Ah, hell. Forgot. Get up there and turn it off. Next to the switch for the running lights."

Robert swung open the door and nimbly lifted himself into the cab just like Bud had shown him, and then sat, and sat, looking at the switches, trying to remember which was for the running lights. Bud watched and waited patiently until Robert found what he was looking for. An exit from the cab and slam of its door confirmed he'd flipped the right one.

"So, where'd you come in from tonight?"

"Well, let's see. Left Flagstaff about sunup. Came through Santa Fe, New Mexico and straight up the I-25 to Wally's... I mean, to your little shed."

"You've been driving all that time?"

"Pretty much. Couple of stops."

"You must be dead tired."

"Probably am. Just don't know it yet."

The fact that Bud had bothered to introduce him to the Peterbilt despite fatigue was not lost on Robert. He re-emphasized how he felt. "I really do appreciate you showing me your rig. I had heard you were someone to avoid. Don't know what they were talking about."

"Ha, yeah. Guess that just shows you. Most people are full of shit. Uh, oh, I think I got you in trouble."

A truck sat on the entry lane, its driver standing by the shed waiting for someone to check him in. Parking the Jeep, Robert said nothing, his hands tense, movements jittery.

"Where the hell you been?" Robert got an ear full upon stepping out of his Jeep. "I've been sitting here for half an hour."

"Sorry."

"Damn right you're sorry. What the hell were you doin'? Sleepin' out there?"

Of course, Bud would intervene, but this driver was unknown to him. He wore a checked, not Pearsall shirt, and Bud figured he was an independent driver in his own tractor dropping a trailer for transfer.

"Hey, mister, it's my fault." Bud approached while Robert did his walk-around. "I had him out in the lot helping me with something."

The man looked at Bud, and then at Robert, deciding to harp on the younger man who appeared less intimidating. "I've got a fucking schedule to keep." He turned away from Bud and moved towards Robert near the back of the trailer. "I don't have time to sit here while you play around. Who is that? Your boyfriend?"

Dropping his duffel bag and paperwork in front of the man's tractor, Bud rounded its corner bumper in the direction of its driver, but stopped when he heard Robert's voice.

"That's right, mister. Why do you ask? Are you jealous?" Robert dropped his inspection clipboard and stood facing his antagonist, their chests one foot apart. "I's giving him a ride in from the lot. You know why? Because the man's been on the road for six days. How 'bout you? Where'd you come from? Laramie? If you're in such a god damned hurry, why don't you shut the fuck up and let me do my job?"

And so, the moment of truth had arrived. Seconds of tension passed, as the angry driver tried to decide whether or not his delay was worth the fight. Was he willing to back up his bitching with fisticuffs? Perhaps he had unleashed a lion in this young man, a savage beast whose inner fire belied his less-than-threatening physique.

Bud was proud that his student had absorbed every word of his teaching. Intimidation worked. The man backed down. "Ah, go ahead. Do your job."

Robert Carlyle was as pleasant as could be in finishing his inspection. "You can drop in row C, slot five. Sign here, please."

Little activity was taking place inside the terminal building. One male dock worker and one female dispatcher were the only humans on the clock. Neither of them were known to Bud; neither of them rushed over to celebrate his triumphant return from near-disaster; neither of them even acknowledged his presence. With the office door locked, Bud dropped his packet and log book through its slot and checked in with the weekend dead time dispatcher, a haggard-looking woman who was reading a paperback book.

"Hi. Any messages for me?"

After a five-second delay, her eyes never leaving printed page, a monotone "You are?" was her greeting.

"Bud Richter."

"No."

"Thanks."

As Bud turned to walk away, she stopped him. "Wait, yes." With book in one hand, she grabbed papers out the "B. Richter" slot and handed them over. Finished with this interruption, she returned to her reading.

"Thanks."

Bud didn't even look at the notes until he got to his Custom Cruiser, parked near the building beyond the highest numbered dock bay. He laid his duffel on the passenger seat, leaving his door open to provide overhead light. All three notes were written in Jenny's hand, which made him wonder if the woman just encountered would bother to write down a message for him if she did receive one. These three were simple: call Julie, "naturally," he thought; call Jenny, "naturally," he thought; call Byron McAfee 677-2000, ext. 243, "don't know that one," he said. None of them would be called at this time of night/morning anyway, so Bud laid the notes aside, started the wagon and made way for the exit lane where Robert sat in his shed.

"That guy still out there?"

"Sure is. He wasn't so tough, was he?"

"Hot air. You handled it like a pro. Sorry I got you in trouble."

"It was worth every minute. Go home, Bud. Your bed's waiting."

The Drunk and the Dead

Bud was still on-call until midnight Sunday, so he slept with his phone on the hook not expecting any interruptions. Not likely that the driver second on seniority list would be bothered for a short-haul run on Sunday. He was in the depths of five hours worth of sleep when the phone rang at seven a.m. It rang six times.

"Mmm... Hello?"

"Bud?"

"Yes."

"This is Jenny. Wake up and listen."

"I'll listen asleep."

"No, Bud. I need to tell you that... Harry had an accident Saturday."

"Yeah. Wally told me the other transmission did what mine did."

"That's what they think, but they're not sure yet."

"Well, what did Harry say?"

"Bud... Harry was killed."

"What?" The line was silent for a few seconds, as Bud sorted out his confusion. "Wait a minute. Wally didn't say anything about that."

"Nobody else knows. I took the call and paged Perry Jacobs. He said to keep it quiet until we know more about what happened."

"I...uh... I..."

Jenny's compassion prompted her to tell Bud everything she did know before allowing him his grief in private. "The Iowa Highway Patrol rep told me Harry went up an exit ramp east of Des Moines, locked the brakes and skidded off the ramp. His tractor crashed head-on into a concrete support column below."

"Why would he... there must have been traffic... he wouldn't have... oh, man, oh man," his voice cracked. "God damn it to hell."

She heard him cover the mouthpiece with his hand. Jenny waited... and waited... until Bud came back on the line. He spoke clearly, and with composure.

"Ok, Jenny. Who is this McAfee guy?"

"Oh, uh..." Bud's sudden shift in subject caught Jenny off guard. She hesitated in order to recall the message. "Um, well, he didn't say. I figured you knew him. If you don't know, then I assume he's with Freightliner... or with their insurance company. He called on Friday."

"Huh... you'd think he would leave a company name or something."

"I don't know, Bud. I didn't press him."

"Well, ok. Are you supposed to work today? If you do maybe you can find out who he is."

"I can't work today."

"Why not? Might be good therapy."

"I am in no mood."

"Ok, then. Let me know if you hear anything."

He clicked off before she could say another word, and it's just as well he did. Jenny seethed. Jenny was dumbfounded. His callous request for *her* to investigate *his* personal phone message under such a cloud of sorrow was inexcusable, the height of arrogance. With no words of thanks to her for going against her boss's orders to share her information, with no words of compassion for her, for the grief that she felt, Bud's lofty status had come crashing down. Jenny's admiration for his free-spirited, fun-loving approach to life did a complete reversal. Bud Richter was a cold-hearted man, no other way to describe him, and she told herself she would never again do anything to please him. As the phone still held in her hand blasted its dead-line, intermittent screeches, she hung up the receiver to rejoin her still-sleeping husband. Jenny nestled next to him, remembering but one phrase from her conversation with Bud -- *Might be good therapy.*

"The hell with him. This is my therapy." Jenny threw back the covers, yanked away George's underwear and rode on him like he was the mighty stallion of her dreams.

Bud stripped away his underwear and showered. Hot, nearly scalding water soothed his neck, shoulders and back, and just as he had always done, Bud Richter internalized his sorrow. He pressed it deep inside him for release at some other time by means of fists or by means of sex or by means of unplanned outbursts of grief. He thought of the irony, of how he had miraculously saved his unit despite barreling down a six degree grade, while Harry had lost his when climbing a ramp. Should it not have been the other way around? Where had the ghosts of the Lincoln Highway been when *Harry* needed them? The Bud Richter therapy took hold, anger replacing grief, a therapy Jennie did not understand.

Bud didn't feel like wearing clothes, so he didn't. Only his ever-available shower sandals could be tolerated. His refrigerator had eggs. He cracked one and did not like the look of it. There was milk, the aroma of which demanded it also be discarded. Coffee was never an issue. He prepared a full twelve cups in his electrical percolator, one of the few wedding presents that ended up in the Bud box instead of the Julie. And then he called Julie.

"Are you coming home? You never did say, Bud. I don't know why you put me through this mystery every time."

"Because it makes you hornier than you already are, that's why."

"Cute. Well, what's the plan? You know Lisa and Jack want to see you."

She always played that angle, and it always worked, not that he would admit such a thing to her. "Bullshit. They're too busy to care about me. I'm coming for you, lady. May not be until Tuesday, though. Monday I'll probably have to see a Freightliner guy... and maybe some insurance guys."

"Why?"

He didn't really want to get into it. But what else could he do? Bud told Julie the Freightliner story, doing his best to calm her down. This having been the first time she had dealt with an on-the-road accident, same as Bud, Julie was confronted with visions of life without Bud, her children without their father, and although she had been through this before when he was overseas, that was ten years ago. This was different. Their relationship had dramatically altered since then. Their physical distance had strengthened their emotional closeness, and although she did her best to suppress it, Julie burst into tears.

How many times had he made her cry? Countless, but until now her tears were caused by her disappointment in him, or her anger with him. Their years together, their years of marriage, were a never-ending battle of unbridled lust versus uncontrolled rage. It wasn't Julie's fault. It wasn't Bud's fault, but it was Bud's anger simmering just beneath the surface that constantly fueled their emotional roller coaster.

Bud's fists were scarred. He had been programmed to use them, but never did he use them on her. The matching scars were in that barn, for this is where he would go when the pain of his childhood, the pain of his own guilt would well up in him. Split boards were proof of his love for her. When arguments reached the boiling point, Bud could always control himself long enough to revisit the surroundings where he suffered most. The fixtures inside the Richter barn -- the dry, weary, grey wood that had witnessed so many times a father beating his son, with switches, with leather, with open hand, with fists -- they now took the brunt of Bud's rage, not Julie. But how much longer could he maintain his control? Fear drove him away from her. The thought of hitting a woman, any woman, was abhorrent to him. And what of his children? Could it be that the evil gene possessed by his father was also planted inside him? The ever-increasing chance that any of them might suffer the power of his wrath was unacceptable. Bud's only remedy was to remove himself from all of them.

"Now, look, Julie. Everything is fine. Not a scratch on me."

"Oh, Bud... damn it... I know... It's just... the thought of..."

"Don't think it. You know I'm invincible. Even if I'm taken some place else, I'll just wait for you." She began to regain control of herself, as Bud helped her. "You're never going to get rid of me, so don't even try."

Julie said nothing, but the seconds between sniffles increased until she was completely silent.

"That sounds better. I'll bet you're real horny now, huh?"

"That's... darn you, Bud... that's not the half of it."

"Good. I thought so. I will call you first thing tomorrow morning. Give you my scheduled time of arrival. Ok?"

"Ok, Bud."

"Talk to you then. Bye, Julie."

"Goodbye, Bud."

With the line dead and Julie unable to know it, Bud agonized, too. Her distant sobs nearly caused him to break, until a warmth brought joy. Emanating from the depths of his chest, it is the heat accurately described as burning desire, for here was a woman who mourned for him. He wasn't dead, not even hurt, yet she sobbed over the unthinkable, the unimaginable. What would she do without him? How could she survive if something happened to him?

He poured a cup of coffee and reclined in his one living room chair adjacent to his one living room couch. He clung to this emotional warmth. No greater gift could be bestowed upon a man. To be presented with a woman such as this, at the time in his life when he was on the verge of killing his father or himself or both; to be presented with a woman who had taught him, waited for him, comforted him, tolerated him, overlooked his other women, satisfied his every need no matter how bizarre, this was a gift from the gods. Bud's protectors, Bud's ghosts, were a powerful force. Nothing could take Bud away from Julie or Julie away from Bud.

In the Bud vernacular, their history was compressed into its simplest form. "Damn, I am one lucky son of a bitch."

With that resolved, he pondered what to do on the Byron McAfee matter. Who was he and would he be answering a telephone on Sunday morning? Bud found Jenny's note and dialed.

"Cheyenne Police Department, Lincolnway Station."

Bud took a few seconds to recover from that one. "Hello... uh, extension 243, please." Now, with a bit of luck the mystery man would be at his desk. He wasn't. Instead, four rings triggered a recorder.

You've reached the desk of Detective Frank Johnson. Please leave your name and number, and your call will be returned as soon as possible..."

Bud recorded his name and phone number and nothing more.

"Great," he thought. His attempt to get answers only resulted in more questions. Freightliner-related? Harry-related? Whatever, Bud began hoping Pearsall would call him in for a short, one-day run just so he would have something else to occupy his mind. The one issue he could address was the rumbling of his stomach, so Bud finished his hygienic duties, dressed and headed out for breakfast.

His favorite nearby eating spot was Bud's Diner -- not because of the name, even Bud wasn't that pompous -- Bud ate here for the food, service and price, because whether on the road or at home, Bud made it his priority to know the best places to eat. Arriving simultaneously with Bud's meal on his table was a police cruiser behind his Custom Cruiser. He watched and ate, as one uniformed officer walked around Bud's car and another wrote down his license plate number. Disgruntled, Bud quickly consumed what he had hoped to enjoy, paid his ticket at the register rather than transacting his business with the waitress, and then exited the restaurant. He approached the police cruiser instead of his own car, as both officers sat inside, the driver talking on the radio with window down.

"Sir, I'm Bud Richter." He pointed to his station wagon. "That's my car."

Bud was not at all pleased that he was made to ride in the police cruiser. The fact that he had made the effort to call Byron McAfee and had left a message for Frank Johnson did not impress the officers. They confirmed his identification, told him to lock up his vehicle and opened their back door for him to sit and ride.

It took great resolve to control his anger when they informed him that they had just been to his residence and knocked on his apartment door, where his neighbors undoubtedly were now gossiping about the criminal living amongst them. Somehow, Bud maintained his composure, exercised civility and remained silent all the way to the Lincolnwood Station. He would save his protests for Detective Johnson or Byron McAfee or whoever instigated this humiliation, depending of course upon the purpose for his abduction.

Both men greeted him at the front desk with name-only introductions and hand shakes before escorting him to a back office, Johnson in the lead, McAfee in the rear.

"Have a seat," said Frank Johnson, a mid-forties, dark-haired and handsome man who stood at least six feet tall with a slightly rounded belly, solid, no jiggling. Black slacks, white long-sleeved shirt with sleeves rolled midway to his forearms and a black necktie completed his purely cop-like appearance.

An already cramped room housed a small desk covered with odd stacks of paper. Johnson took his seat behind it, while Bud and McAfee filled the remaining two chairs positioned close together in front. Byron McAfee's casual knit shirt and jeans belied Detective Johnson's typical detective garb, but he too was a law enforcer, appearing in age to be at least ten years younger than his partner.

"Mr. Richter," Johnson spoke. "Detective McAfee is with the Sacramento Police Department, in California."

"I was just there."

"Yes, we know," McAfee enlightened his interviewee. "We understand you had an argument with a woman in back of Hank's Truck Plaza."

"It wasn't much of an argument. She wouldn't let go of my arm, so I pushed her away like this." Bud demonstrated, repeating the minimal force of his thrust. "She was so drunk she stumbled and fell."

"Why was she hanging onto you?"

Innocent men tell the truth, regardless of sordid activities. "She's a prostitute, a trucker's hag. She offered a blow job or screw for a price. I took the blow job option and gave her... ten dollars, as I recall. But when she tried to get into my sleeper, she fell backwards and I caught her. That's when I knew she's drunk or doped up or something, and I cancelled the deal. Told her to keep the money. But she didn't want to cancel. She grabs my arm and starts begging me to let her suck my dick. I didn't get it. She had her money. Whatever, I showed you what happened. Why? Is she saying I did something else?"

"What happened next?" McAfee ignored Bud's question.

"Well, I offered my hand to help her get up. Asked her if she was ok."

"Did you help her get up?"

"No, she wouldn't let me. Got herself up and told me to get away from her."

"And then?"

"And then, nothing. She staggered back over towards the restaurant."

"What did you do?"

"I got into my sleeper, locked the door and jacked off. Then I went to sleep."

"Mr. Richter, we found semen in the cab of your truck."

"So? I just told you I jacked off. It's my semen, ain't it? Wait a minute. When were you in my truck?"

"This morning."

"What the hell's going on here?"

"The woman's body was found in a storage tank behind the parking lot."

One of the Good Guys

At this point, innocence had nothing to do with it. Neither of these detectives had given Bud that *anything you say can and will be used against you* speech, but that is exactly what Bud heard rattling in his brain. He heard nothing else, and even though he knew he could prove his innocence if given a few moments alone to figure it out, he also knew he'd best not try to do that.

"Well, gentlemen, I suggest you call my boss. I don't hear you charging me with any crime, but until I talk to him, I don't think I'll be talking to you."

Frank Johnson turned the phone in Bud's direction. "Here, you call him."

"I've gotta get his home number out of my wallet." Bud dialed. Twelve rings got no answer.

"Can you page him?" Johnson asked.

"Yeah, let me try that. What number do I put in?"

Perry Jacobs came through the main switchboard within three minutes, routed directly to the extension displayed on his pager.

"Frank Johnson."

"This is Perry Jacobs."

"Mr. Jacobs, one of your drivers is here to speak with you. Bud Richter. Hold on."

"Perry?"

"What's going on, Bud?"

"I need you down here. They're holding me on murder charges."

"What? Where?"

"Lincolnway Station, off Catalpa."

"I'll be right there."

Detectives Johnson and McAfee were a bit agitated with their guest, which was exactly Bud's intent. Plus, he figured that would get Jacobs to move at double speed.

"Now, Mr. Richter," Johnson explained. "We have not charged you with anything."

"Then why am I still here?"

"You saw this woman," McAfee joined in. "We are looking for any information that could be helpful."

"If that's true, then you sure got funny ways of going about it." Bud licked his lips, preparing to vent that long-suppressed protest.

"How so?"

"First of all. You didn't have to send officers knocking on my door where I have to live, tracking me down at my favorite restaurant where everybody knows me. I called your office this morning. It's not like I was avoiding you. Had Byron McAfee bothered to say who he was and the purpose of the call when he left his message, I would have called you as soon as I hit town last night. No, you had to be tricky about it. Why the hell couldn't I have followed the officers in my car? Or they could have followed me? No, you've got to make me leave my car unattended in a business parking lot and cart me down here as though I was going to run away. What if my car gets towed? Or vandalized? Are you going to reimburse me? Excuse me, gentlemen, it's insulting. But hell, I understand. I'm just a stupid truck driver. What do I know about proper procedures? We'll just intimidate him into saying something to incriminate himself. Look, I got nothing to hide, fellas, but if you think you're gonna trick me into saying I did something I didn't do, you've got the wrong stupid truck driver."

Both detectives remained cool and methodical, as Johnson answered his phone, telling the caller to "bring him on back."

"Mr. Richter," Johnson took the lead. "We apologize if we have slighted you in our methods."

"It was never our intention to insult you," McAfee added with a hint of sarcasm most men might have missed. Not Bud.

"Well, you failed miserably, detective. Why didn't you just tell me right off the bat the woman was dead? Huh? Telling me about witnesses seeing me with her and all this beating around the bush. I've been all over this country, pal. I've always been straight with law men, as long as they're straight with me. California, Arkansas, it don't matter. Either you're a stand-up man or you ain't. I served my country. Twice, god damn it. Did you do a background on me? I doubt it."

The opening of the door and entrance of Perry Jacobs did nothing to interrupt Bud's dramatic speech. "I'm one of the good guys. Ok? So don't treat me like I'm some kind of career criminal... and don't think I'm some hick fresh in from the corn field who doesn't have a clue about your little game."

"Bud? What's happening?" Perry delayed any detective response to Bud's venting, but he didn't wait for Bud to answer him before addressing the other two. "What is this man charged with?"

Frank Johnson rose from his desk with hands on hips. "Nothing, sir. We just needed to ask..."

"Good," Bud cut him off. "Then let me talk to my boss in private. Then maybe we'll continue and maybe we won't."

Both Johnson and McAfee left the room, closing the door behind them. "Bud, what in the world is going on?"

Bud put his index finger to his own lips, indicating for Perry to shut up. He pointed to the open space beneath the door, where shadows of feet darkened the gap of light. He looked around the room, found a wooden ruler and poked it under the door. "Hey! Do we get our privacy or not?"

As the shadows disappeared, Bud doubled over with laughter.

"Come on, Bud," Perry's curiosity was in no mood for joking around. "Fill me in."

"God almighty... I cannot believe those two clowns."

"Bud, please. Cut this shit out and tell me."

The story was told, quietly, in detail, from the time Bud pulled into Hank's Truck Plaza until the time he picked up his trailer in Bakersfield.

"Well, we've got records. The times you called us. Your log book. Whatever. Think you can remember the employees at Hank's you talked to?"

"Sure. I never forget a face, no matter how ugly."

"Bud. This could be serious. Did they tell you if they've determined her time of death?"

"No. I've been chewing their ass out ever since I got off the phone with you. Oh, by the way... did you know they searched the BXM tractor this morning?"

"No."

"Do you suppose they bothered to get a warrant? If they didn't, you ought to sue their pants off."

"Well, you better just cool it. I'm going to call our law firm. I imagine we can cooperate with them, but not until our attorney gets here. Are they holding you?"

"Not as far as I know"

"No charges?"

"Nope."

"Let me page Harvey... get him down here."

Harvey Mickle, from the law firm of Brown, Mickle, and Jamison responded within six minutes, joining his clients within twenty. In between, Frank Johnson and Byron McAfee were told the private conversation had not ended, even though it had, and they both turned around to leave the room. Another good chuckle for Bud.

He never asked his boss about Harry, because he wasn't supposed to know. Why it was such a big secret was unknown, but he didn't care. If

Perry wished it, then Bud accepted.

With two detectives, one truck driver, one truck line office manager and one attorney gathered in a Cheyenne police station conference room, it was determined that any future information gathered by the two detectives would come from their own investigative work. Since Byron McAfee refused to grant Bud any sort of immunity from prosecution, they were forced to obtain search warrants for access to the Pearsall Truck Lines dispatcher logs, Bud's driving log, Bud's duffel bag, which he left untouched for their inspection. Inside, they found his dirty white sock encrusted with Bud's semen, which lab tests proved was of a vintage very near to the time he'd said he jacked off, which was one of many factors that when put together excluded him from any further suspicion.

Harvey Mickle, at the request of Perry Jacobs, filed a formal complaint against the Cheyenne Police Department for their warrantless search of the BXM tractor, not to mention their unlawful entrance onto the Pearsall lot.

For allowing them entry, young Robert Carlyle's employment was terminated, until Bud intervened.

"Come on, Perry. Was he trained on how to handle that situation? You know damned good and well he wasn't. Hell, Wally would have done the same thing if he'd been on duty, so you know he never told the kid about search warrants and what the police can and cannot do. Those two snowballed Robert the way they tried to do me. Give him a break."

Break granted. In fact, Robert was sent to the loading docks for a better paying position with a little action to it. "Put him on the three to eleven shift for starters," Bud suggested. "Let him get used to what's happening when it's not so busy."

Rarely did Perry Jacobs ignore the advice of Bud Richter, and this was certainly not the first time Perry had come to Bud's rescue. Both men had a knack for quickly recognizing good character versus bad. It's the reason Perry had taken a chance on hiring Bud in the first place. Recently divorced, recently and honorably discharged from the service, after just having been released from the VA Hospital for short-term physical injuries and long-term mental, after just having buried his father, and with no commercial driving experience other than vehicles used on the farm or for war, Bud came looking for a new life and new career. Sitting opposite Perry's desk was a broken man. Perry sensed it despite Bud's best efforts to hide it. More than this, Perry sensed a man of quality, a man of loyalty, so Perry took a chance on Bud and his judgment paid off handsomely.

He worked Bud in slowly, assigning Bud to hostler duties in the yard, allowing Bud to practice with a trailer in tow on his own time, until Bud was ready to make short-haul runs of single-day or one-overnight lengths. Once on the road for good, Bud quickly became one of Pearsall's stellar drivers, always keeping his schedules, logs and equipment in perfect order, always done with the utmost of courtesy and professionalism. He never called in sick, never failed a drug or alcohol screening. In other words, Bud Richter was a man who never caused Perry Jacobs any headaches, and for a truck line office manager, this is a precious gift. It is why Perry immediately responded to Bud's page and got to the police station as soon as possible. Bud in trouble was a rarity, and Perry knew Bud's call for help was for good reason.

As for Robert, Bud's opinion was all Perry needed to hear. Bud's good word meant that the youthful Robert Carlyle would flower to become a valuable asset to the company. End of discussion.

Bud's Lament
(with whiskey chaser)

Everybody said I's crazy for going back over there, especially as a Marine. "Man," they said. "You'll never make it on the ground. Things are different. Men are dying every day. You did your Viet Nam service. Why would you go back?"

They didn't understand. I had to get out of here. Had to get away from dirt... from cow shit... from my old man. Couldn't see any other way to do it. Figured nothing could be worse than trying to work with a man I wanted to kill every minute of every day.

Can't say it was right... can't say it was wrong. Sure, I saw some fucked up shit. I did some fucked up shit. Got used to seeing swollen bodies float down the Ben Hai River. Men, women, children... didn't matter... didn't stop me and my buddy Marshall from taking our dip... washing away our sweat with muck. We just stayed out of their way.

He was a Michigan boy. I was an old man to him... ha... twenty-four... old man. Didn't take us long to get in synch. He knew what I was thinking without me saying a word. Same for me with him. We knew the moves we were gonna make just by our body language.

Speaking of water, that's what we did. We brought it up the hill to the camps near the DMZ. Wells were down below. Had to do it in the daytime. Wide open to take bullets... or mortar. Marshall and I had to be in synch, every second, if we wanted to do our job and live. That's not to say we never ran into people to kill. Had to after we saw a buddy blown up while trying to help some kid. Kid blew himself up. From then on, any native coming near us had to get away or die. And I mean *anybody*. Had to die. How do you know? You can't. They made the rules, not us. They're the ones who sent kids out to be walking death traps, not us. You don't think about it. Else it'll eat out your insides.

Surviving that was nothing compared to coming back here. Why did I? Had to... wife and two kids waiting. Sure as hell wasn't like when I came home the first time. In '67 people around here were proud of me, or at least they said they were. In '70, they acted like I'd caused it. Like I'd started the fiasco of Viet Nam myself, personally.

Worst of it was those punks from high school... Harold Turley... Ronnie Stover... that gang. Fuckers live in a time warp. Still wearing their

103

class rings, for god sakes, like high school was the highlight of their worthless lives. Pissed 'em off when I beat Harold out as the starting running back. Ha, made him play full back... had to block for me. Did a piss poor job, too, so coach made him play defense. Stover hated having to give me the ball, but what could he do? Coach called the plays. Had to do it if we wanted to win. Everybody wanted to win except for those two. They were all about Harold and Ronnie and their little pea-brained clan of nitwits.

Oh, well, they got even... for awhile... when I's down... too down to fight back... calling me soldier boy... baby killer. Didn't have time to deal with their shit. Old man was laid up... had a stroke... up to me to turn a profit so me and my family could eat.

Back into the dirt... into the cow shit. Old man could hardly talk, but he still kept badgering me. Everything I did, I did it wrong... Cock sucker. I couldn't slap him down like I used to... poor old cripple... I kept telling him to hurry up and die, you old piece of crap. You ain't worth the air you're breathing, so why are you still here?

Think I'm a cold-hearted son of a bitch, don't ya. Look at me like I'm crazy... you're damn right I'm crazy.

Tell it to me when I was six years old and he was beatin' the crap outta me... because I didn't get my work done... because he expected me to do the work of four. Yeah, he wanted four sons but only got me and my three sisters... that was my fault. Tell it to me when I's crying every night, wondering why my mother and my sisters pretended like nothing was happening... wondering how come none of the other boys had to make sure all their bruises were covered up when they went to school.

Rotten mother fucker... he's lucky I didn't kill him when he *was* healthy. He found out... 'bout the time I turned thirteen he found out... bull rushed him... took us both through barbed wire fence... cut us both to pieces... then I gave him seven years worth of 'oomph,' stomps to his chest... and 'aargh,' kicks to his ribs... ha... then he had to cover up his scars... never fucked with me again... still tried to fuck with my head though... still thought I's gonna take orders from him... 'til I'd slap him down like the bitch he was. Hard-headed old fool never did learn... even when I's a grown man... back from the Navy. Some men just gotta get beat... that's all there is to it... nothing to talk about... they just gotta get beat to a bloody pulp.

God, how Julie suffered. Any little thing she did would set me off. Trivial shit, harmless shit, now that I think back on it.

Hell, she was naive... never been anywhere outside Phillips County. Who's fault was that? Mine. She waited for me twice and forever to get the crap out my brain. After I finally talked the old man into dying, that was it. I had to fly... to save myself... to save Julie and my kids... from me.

Perry Jacobs is my hero. Always will be. He took a chance on me. Gave me a purpose. My purpose was to never fail him. Still is. That's how I keep from failing myself... from failing Julie and Lisa and Jack. He never had to do that. He didn't know me... didn't owe me a damn thing. He... ah, shit... hold on... Hey, lemme tell you somethin'. That man restored me. Perry Jacobs is my hero. Period.

The Cherry Pie Argument

Bud got his wish. His busy Sunday kept his mind off of Harry Preston, at least until he got home around seven that night. He had decided to eat where Perry dropped him off to pick up his car -- Bud's diner.

Bud asked Perry to join him, offered to purchase his meal for saving him from the big, bad, Cheyenne police, but Perry declined in favor of his wife's home cooking. As for Bud, he used the opportunity to entertain the diner employees with his tale of intrigue while filling his long-neglected belly at the same time.

Once home, he took his duffel from the bedroom and set it near the door, touching nothing inside that hadn't already been removed -- his shower sandals, shaving bag and Jimmy's tape. The duffel would go with him to the Pearsall terminal on Monday, his day off, to be made available if and when a warrant was produced for its inspection. Harvey Mickle would be on guard to watch every move made by Detectives Johnson and McAfee.

He showered. Somehow the smell of a police station didn't sit well with him. He tried to watch the evening news, but fell asleep in his recliner. Just before midnight he awoke and transferred himself to his bed, and by eight a.m. he was in the Pearsall terminal, standing at Jenny's station.

"Any news about Harry?" Bud whispered.

"No. Perry's going to make the announcement around ten. Then it will be posted throughout the building for the late shifts."

"Did they bring his body back yet?"

"Bud, I don't know any more today than I did yesterday."

Seems as though Jenny was a bit agitated, so Bud dropped that subject. "Have you heard anything from Freightliner?"

"Bud, I told you..."

"No, no... I mean do they want to interview me about *my* accident, because if they don't, I'm outta here."

"Going home, are you?"

"Home, sweet home."

"Fine. That's a good place for you. Let me call them and see if they want you. I know I don't."

"Aw, you're breaking my heart," he said. "Damn woman, chill out," he thought. Bud sauntered off towards the office while Jenny made the call. Finding Perry, he handed over his duffel. "Don't open that. It's gotta be ripe in there."

"Don't worry. I'll let Harvey do that. We're paying him for it."

Perry told Bud of the police department's illegal search, and of Robert's firing, which led to Robert's rehiring.

"Hey, Perry, what's going to happen with that BXM tractor?"

"We're going to piggyback it to Salt Lake."

"When?"

"Uh, probably Thursday. Got to wait for the police to decide if they're going to look through it again. Soon as they release it, I'll try to get a load set up from Salt Lake to here so we make some money off the deal."

"Maybe you can get a load from here to there. Make some money that way."

"And how the hell will our driver get back?"

"Oh, duh... that's why I drive and you consign. Why don't you just buy the damned thing?"

"It's four years old, Bud."

"So? Did you look at it? That thing is pristine. Check the hours on it. Bet there aren't any. Old ain't always bad, Perry. Your precious Freightliners proved that."

"Maybe I will buy it, just for you. Would that make you happy?"

"No, just give me back Matilda. I don't give a shit about the rest of it."

Perry's secretary appeared to inform Bud that Jenny was transferring a call. He took it in Perry's office.

"Mr. Richter, we'd like to talk with you about the Freightliner tractor... you know, how it acted before and after the failure."

"You coming here?"

"We'll send a man."

"I'm off the clock until Thursday late. How long will it take?"

"One, maybe two hours at the most. Tell me a time and I'll set it up."

"Thursday afternoon at four. I'll be in the terminal's main office."

"Very good. I'll call with our representative's name as soon as I know who it will be."

"I'll be here. Thank you."

Bud bounced from Perry's office. "Hey, partner. I'm outta here, unless you say otherwise."

"No. If the cops need you they'll have to wait for... when?"

"Thursday. Gotta see a Freightliner man at four."

"Bud. I need to tell you something."

"And what's that?" As though Bud didn't know what was coming.

"Harry Preston was killed Saturday outside of Des Moines."

Bud pretended to be shocked, standing with eyes moist while Perry told it all. There was new information Bud hadn't heard, direct from the Iowa Highway Patrol to Perry.

"Skid marks showed that Harry locked up the brakes and then released them. There was a gap, and then a second series of skid marks that swerved off the ramp. Their theory is that Harry abandoned his attempt to stop his rig because there was a line of cars waiting at the stop sign. It extended down the ramp. Witnesses said that rather than plow into them, Harry took his rig off the ramp. He crashed into a concrete support column holding up the bridge. Killed him right then and there."

Genuine moisture framed Bud's eyes, as he collected himself to respond. "Hell of a thing, ain't it? That was Harry... he was a lot more than people know."

"We know. Don't we, Bud."

"Damn right." The two men stood facing one another four feet apart, both with identically glistening eyes, both with identically upturned mouths -- right side only and ever so slight, a cocky smirk, a nodding of the head, an expression of mutual recognition, and of remembrance.

"What about the funeral, Perry?"

"Don't know yet."

"I'll be at Julie's. Call me when you know."

"Will do, Bud. First thing."

Bud thought it appropriate that thundershowers followed him from Cheyenne to Holyoke. It was a good day to be sad, at least until he got to Julie's house. The down side was that with rain, the social club would more than likely be contaminating the Koffee Kup Kafe, taking up space with their moronic drivel. They were. Harold Turley's monster-sized Lincoln was parked in front of the door, over the line and taking two spaces.

It was just past ten a.m. and all the serious people had come to eat and gone to work, but the back table was busy. All went silent and Bud ignored them.

"Good morning, Maggie."

"Hi, Bud."

"How's Greg?"

"Doing fine. He ran over to the bank for a bit."

"Tell him hi for me. Whatcha got left?"

"There's still blackberry, apple, raisin and chocolate."

"You didn't save me a cherry? Julie's not gonna like that."

"Sorry, Bud. Sold the last one to Har... " Maggie knew she had blundered. "Harold."

Most times Bud wouldn't pester them as long as they kept quiet while he was in there, but today he was feeling a bit cocky, what with his brilliant saving of doomed vehicle and masterful dismantling of two police detectives. He turned his head slowly, looked with disbelief at the four men who each were enjoying a slice of Maggie pie, and then returned his gaze to Maggie.

"Mrs. Deitrich, do you mean to tell me that Harold Turley actually made a purchase in your café? Other than sucking on coffee all day?"

Maggie tilted her head with a sneer that said, 'Bud, give it a rest,' and nodded yes.

"Well, I'll be god damned." Bud rested one elbow on the counter and faced the back table. "Must be expectin' a bumper crop this year, for Harold to shell out all that money. How about it, Harold? This rain doin' you some good?"

Turley sat down his fork, took a slow slip of coffee, gently set the mug onto the table. "I love cherry pie. Thought I'd better take this one before some rag head beat me to it."

It was a rare thing for Bud not to have a come-back, but that one totally threw him for a loop, especially when Harold, Ronnie and the other two burst into laughter.

Bud looked at Maggie. "What the hell is he talking about?"

"Don't know, Bud."

He shook his head in puzzlement. "Why, Harold, I think you're crazier than I am." Bud turned to the counter. "Maggie, give me the blackberry and the chocolate."

Transaction completed, Bud was content to leave things as they were, but apparently Harold was also feeling cocky. As Bud reached for the door with his back turned to their table, Harold made a play for the last word.

"Tell Julie she'll have to make her own cherry pie. She oughtta have plenty of time, since her man's never around."

"Now, look here, Harold." Bud turned to face them, setting his pies on a nearby table. "Have you forgotten the night over at Joe's Tavern? Right over there? How I tried to beat some sense into you? And you, Ronnie, and your long-gone pal, Charlie Hofstra?"

None of the four moved, none cowered and none spoke, except for Harold. "Sure, Bud, we remember it. I reckon you remember a time before that, don't ya?"

"Sure, I remember. Difference is, I faced you all like a man. Told you exactly what I was gonna do and did it. Ain't the same as sneaking up from behind, catching a man when he's down."

In Bud's own barn in 1971, that's when and where Harold, Ronnie and the other two were waiting, and when Bud came storming in filled with rage from another nightly argument with Julie, they jumped him. So heated was that night's row with his wife that Bud failed to notice the incessant barking of his hunting dogs from their pen nearby. He didn't see the car parked on his property that didn't belong. So close to striking her that night, Bud had run from the house in his underwear to unleash his fists on the dead, rather than the living.

The very same four men with whom he now argued had no trouble that night in subduing a man depressed, drunk, angry and unsuspecting, and they proceeded to beat his gut to smithereens. Harold's request. Told them to, "punch him like his old man used to do." Only the belly, no face, so all bruises could be hidden. Two men held one arm apiece locked in half-nelsons, pulled them behind Bud's head, while Harold and Ronnie took turns driving their fists into him. He puked. They let him drop, waited, and then stood him up to continue. They intended injury, permanent, organ-rupturing damage, and would have done so had there not been intervention. The barking of Richter dogs instigated barking from the neighbor's dogs, the Chalmers, and it was Wilton and his father who saved Bud, speaking more with two shotguns than with words. After the four attackers reluctantly drove away, Wilton and his dad took Bud to the hospital in Julesburg, and from there he was transferred to the Veteran's Administration hospital in Cheyenne.

Bud remembered, and as he stared down the four men who'd caused him this grief, he burst into laughter. "Yeah, funny how that worked out, ain't it? Thanks to you, the VA got me on a program. Got my brain fixed, so you couldn't fuck with me anymore. Yeah, thanks to you, I've been able to keep you rats down in the gutter where you belong. Make sure you remember that you've got shit for brains and nothing will ever change it. Every time I see you I'm gonna remind you. And if words don't keep you down, then I'll beat you down like I did already. John? Bill? You ain't got yours yet. You lucked out staying home, instead of tagging along with these two to Joe's. But I haven't forgot. I will do it again, so help me god, one at a time or all four of you at once. I'll do it drunk or sober. It don't matter. Don't you *ever* speak to me about Julie. I will beat you 'til you can't see straight."

Bud picked up his pies. "Maggie, I'm sorry." He exited her restaurant, but after setting the pies in his car, he returned to stand in the pouring rain at the eight-foot, plate-glass window. Locking eyes with Harold, Bud pointed to his crotch while mouthing the words, "Bite me," and then waited to see if any of them cared to join him on the sidewalk. They didn't. Harold and his cronies chose to laugh from the safety of their back wall table.

"Damn it, Harold," Maggie scolded. "Why don't you leave him alone?"

"Hey, he started it."

"No, you started it twenty years ago. Over football. How ridiculous! High School is long past, for goodness sakes. Can't you get over it?"

"Football had nothing to do with it."

"Oh, that's right. Your dad started it with his dad thirty-five years ago. And Greg's dad and every other German family around here, like they were Nazis because of their heritage. Probably grandfathers, too. I don't remember. I'm sure they were labeled as Huns. Most of their ancestors were here before yours were, Harold. They're as American as can be."

"You oughtta know. You married one of 'em."

"That's right. Greg served this country. So did Bud. Twice. Did you? No. You stayed home. Family hardship. Their fathers got by without them. Why couldn't yours?"

Greg Dietrich burst in soaking wet, returning from his bank deposit errand and none too pleased that his wife was in a fit. "What's going on?"

"Oh, Bud was in here," Maggie explained with voice cracking. "How many years do I have to put up with this useless squabbling? I am so sick of it." She ran to the back room to shed her tears in private.

"What happened, Harold?"

"Richter started mouthing off. What else is new?"

"I thought we had an agreement. I'd let you sit in here and drink coffee all day if you'd leave Bud alone."

"I ain't gonna sit here and let him talk shit to me."

"Damn it, Harold. You know he's not right. Can't you overlook him?"

"Not anymore."

"Well, if you can't keep quiet for the few minutes it takes for him to get his pies and get out... then... then you can get out. I don't need it."

"You're kicking me out of your Kraut restaurant?"

"You broke the agreement. You're bad for business. You've got to go."

Harold stood. His robots mimicked. "Come on, fellas. This shit they call food ain't fit for dogs to eat." He grabbed his plate, held it level with his chest, and dropped it to the floor. Ronnie Stover and the other two did the same.

"You going to make me call Wes?" Greg picked up the phone, threatening to dial.

112

"Sheriff's on our side, Greg. You oughtta know that." Harold slowly walked towards the door near to where Greg stood on the customer side of the counter. "But you oughtn't to bother him. We're leavin'." He poked his index finger into Greg's sternum. "Take my advice, Dietrich. Watch your backside. You and your loony tunes pal, Bud... you both better keep your eyes open."

Greg's only concern was Maggie, and as soon as the last man exited his restaurant, he ran to her. She sat on a stool near a sink full of used, soaking-in-soapy-water dishes. Crying time was over but her eyes were still red, as was her face.

Greg knelt before her and took her hands into his. "You ok?"

"Yes. Are you?"

"Good enough. How are we gonna survive without Harold's seventy-five cents every day?"

"Oh, Greg." She cradled the back of his head, coaxing him to lay it on her lap. "It's just as well. Harold and his gang aggravate our good customers as much as they do me." Maggie stroked her husband's cheek with one hand, his hair with the other. "I get so tired of hearing them talk about nothing... act like they own the place. Won't miss it at all."

"Me neither." He placed his hands on her hips, then wrapped his arms around the small of her back. "I should have kicked their freeloading butts out of here long ago."

"It was my fault. I stupidly told Bud that Harold... oh, Greg, why is it always Bud? Sometimes I feel so sorry... well, you know."

"Yes, Maggie. I do know. Julie never gave you a chance, did she?"

"Lucky for me, I guess. I never could have put up with him like she has."

"No, lucky me. You had to settle for second best."

"Second best? Don't be silly. You swept me off my feet, Greg Dietrich. I gave up my Bud fantasies long ago. Too much clutter... too much hair."

Greg unwrapped and stood, bringing Maggie with him, pulling her close to him for a squeeze. "Hey, lady. Think we've got time for a quickie before the lunch crowd gets here?"

"I wish. You should have asked me before we wasted all that time talking." After a kiss for her husband, Maggie plunged both hands into the dish water. "Go on. Clean up your mess. I'll clean you up after lunch."

Fem Fist Books

Turret Two

"Bastards aren't gonna ruin my day." Bud let off steam as he turned onto the 385 to head south. His hair, face, bare arms and clothing dripped with rainwater, and his steam fogged the windshield. He maxed the defroster fan and opened the glove box for some paper towels, kept there for the same purpose as those kept in his Pearsall tractor. They're always good for something.

Turning onto Richter Road, Bud's spirits were lifted as the clouds broke and sun peeked through. Still, he found reason to grumble. "Great. Dirt road's all mud. What a fine mess this is gonna be."

Elsie was there. No more hunting dogs. Elsie was a serious, property protecting threat to anyone who didn't belong. Julie was on the porch, just like always. "Oh, Bud, you brought your old duffel bag."

"Yep."

"I bought you that when you left for the Navy."

"Looks good as new. Don't you think?"

"You don't. My god, your clothes are soaked."

"Yeah." Bud threw back his arms, thrust out his chest. "See my tits?"

"Not good enough." She hugged and kissed him despite his wetness. "Come on in and get naked. I'll throw your clothes in the dryer."

Bud sat in the buff to consume his nearly-noon breakfast. "Kids doing ok?"

"Sure. It's first of May. They're thinking summer vacation."

"Hard to believe. Do they have a full day today?"

There was no mystery to the point of this question. "Yes, Bud. The house is ours."

"I need a session."

"Oh... ok." Julie was hoping to start Bud off in their bed where she could cradle him, pamper him, let him know how thankful she was that she hadn't lost him to a bad transmission in Utah. But her stronger desire was to please him, and if this is how he wanted her to welcome him home then so be it. Besides, she'd have him where she wanted him sooner or later, sometime before he left her again. "What did you do this time?"

"Well, let's see. Wrecked a truck, killed a woman in Sacramento and argued with Turley at the Kup."

"Damn it, Bud. Why can't you two... wait a minute... what was that about Sacramento?"

"Ha, thought that might get your attention."

Bud dramatized his tale, taking great joy in his clever play at the Cheyenne police station, and by the time his story was finished, his after-meal slice of blackberry pie was halfway gone. "And the kicker to the whole thing? They're doing their investigation right now, while I'm sitting here naked a hundred miles away.

She wanted to admonish him for toying with the police, for once again stirring trouble with Harold, but Julie had learned to save her scoldings as ammunition, as dialogue to be used when it mattered. "Bud, this Sunday is Mother's Day."

"And?" He knew what was coming.

"And, are you going to see her?"

"Yes, before I go back." He no longer gave her his speech of how his mother didn't know who he was, that she wasn't here, only her body was here, so why bother going to see her, she'd just stare blankly and drool like always. Julie had heard it all before, but insisted he visit anyway. Sometimes he would agree to it and sometimes he wouldn't.

"Bud, do you want me to go with you?"

"No, you go see her if you want. I'll stop on my way out of town."

"Where do you want to do this?"

"My weight room. I'm going to shower away this sour first."

"I'll get the dishes."

The northwest, upstairs turret was Bud's room, door always locked, his in-possession key and one more locked in the basement file cabinet the only two in existence. It housed weightlifting equipment -- benches, plates, dumb bells and bar bells. It housed boxing equipment -- lace-up gloves on the floor in one interior corner. Above them and five feet from the corner, a heavy bag hung from a metal spring, which was hooked to a metal plate that was bolted to a main horizontal support beam hidden beneath ceiling plaster. A Bud-constructed chin-up bar also was housed in this room. Anchored by two blocks of wood, two metal bars rose vertically eight feet in height, where they were Bud-welded to a horizontal crossbeam five feet in length.

Nothing in this room would arouse anyone's curiosity, until Bud brought from his basement a pair of file-cabinet hidden cuffs, foam-padded inside, black metal outside, with one link of chain Bud-welded to their centers. Connected to the link on each cuff were spring-loaded eye hooks. Each cuff was released for opening by way of metal fold-over snaps, taken from a pair of rubber galoshes. Opposite to each side of snaps were hinges which allowed the cuffs to open and close around the wrists, snaps snapped to lock them shut.

With cuffs in hand, wearing red gym shorts and black shower sandals, Bud unlocked and entered his room, attending each of the six windows to pull down their shades. Julie was in her bedroom, the northeast turret, undressing when Bud called to her.

"I'm ready."

He had secured the left cuff himself. She did the right, and he jumped to grasp the horizontal crossbeam with his hands. Using one of Bud's flat benches, Julie stood higher to reach the cross beam. Holding on with his left hand, Bud moved his right hand higher and Julie hooked his cuff to the beam through the eye hook. As Bud released his left hand to hang from the eye hook on his right, she repeated the process to leave him suspended by his cuffs, his wrists three feet apart.

Now, only Julie on the bench could release him from the cross beam. She closed the door, and then removed his sandals, leaving his feet bare ten inches above the wood floor.

"Gloves?"

"Yes." Bud brought up his knees, crunching them as close to his stomach as the thickness of his thigh muscles would allow, while Julie put on the boxing gloves. She waited, not bothering to lace them. Twenty leg lifts were followed by stationary lifts, legs straight, feet together and held horizontal to create a forty-five-degree angle. Bud held his legs for a count of twenty seconds before slowly lowering them to vertical. He repeated this pattern ten times, followed by another set of twenty leg lifts, followed by another set of stationary lifts. His body sweat; his abdominal muscles burned, pumped full of blood.

He dropped his legs. He sucked in air. His gym-shorts waistband hung just above his pelvic bone, having worked its way low during his exercises. He winked and tightened his gut to receive her blows.

"You arrogant son of a bitch." She drove the padded glove of a straight right hand into the pit of his stomach. Forward motion met pumped muscle with a resounding thud. "You stuck-up bastard." Her left glove hooked into his belly, just to the right of his navel. A succession of blows was peppered with verbal degradation. "You fucking," right hook... "think you're hot shit," left jab... "piece of crap," straight right. "I will show you who's tough," two from the left... "cut you down to size," a right-left combo... "gonna make you puke," a right upper cut in the gap between navel and waistband.

Julie was trained. Although she possessed no great strength, Bud had shown her how to turn her gloves just before impact, how to use her feet and the pivot of her body for power.

Bud's belly was also trained. Whether at home or on the road, he religiously burned away fat and tightened muscle with crunching exercises, vowing he would never allow himself to fall victim to the trucker's gut, the untamed beach ball of jelly hanging over down-to-the-crotch belt line. This was the public reason for his hard belly. Private reasons, known but to him and Julie also came into play. Never again would he be vulnerable to sneak attack. Bud swore that Turley's knuckles would break before he did, if they ever tried it again.

But mostly, sounds were the main attraction. Initially, only the deep thuds of padded glove versus meaty muscle were heard, but as his abdominal cavity gradually softened with each blow, faint grunts of "oomp" and "ugh" escaped from his throat to accompany impact. Sweat darkened his hair, highlighted his muscle. Sweat brightened her skin, highlighted her curves. His masculine resistance excited her. Her dominating attempts to penetrate excited him.

As Julie ended her first series of blows, Bud collapsed, relaxing all muscles while sucking in air. She allowed his body to hang and recuperate while mocking him.

"Some men just never learn." She paced in front. "How many times? Why do you make me beat you? She removed her gloves. "I told you not to screw with my neighbors." She bare-fisted a right to his belly button. "Now you want to fuck with the police?" She left-hooked the meat above his waistband. "Bring them down on me, too?" She planted her left hand to the small of his back. Pulled him towards her. Formed a claw with her right hand and dug her fingers into the muscled perimeter of his navel. "Who do you think you are?" She buried her fingertips into him with all her strength, eliciting a deep-throated groan from her victim, as he tightened his belly to hold her back. "When will you learn not to mess with me? Don't you know what I'll do to you? Don't you care? Why can't you... why... oh, god... Bud."

Julie released her belly claw and buried her face into him. She frantically licked his briny sweat, kissed his wall of brick, drilled her tongue into his navel. His hard penis sprang upwards to slap her chin when she yanked down his shorts. Her tongue found his dangling testicles, removing their wet salt, replacing it with wet spit. Her tongue laid a trail from his ball sac to the shaft of his peter. It continued to the sensitive triangle of skin beneath his corona. Her touch triggered an involuntary leap of his tool, as it suddenly sprang upwards, nearly making contact with his belly. Upon its return, she engulfed his corona, imprisoning him with her lips, crushing him between her tongue and roof of mouth. He shuddered in her warm vise. He twitched as she drew her lips near to him, slowly consuming his shaft until lips met pubic hair.

"Julie?"

She spit him out, not knowing whether to be agitated or eager.

"Elsie's barking. Hear it?"

She listened. "Yes. Let me see." She tugged an edge of window shade to view the front yard. "Damn it. There's a car coming."

"Where?"

"Just now turning onto the drive."

"Who is it?"

"Don't know, Bud."

"Come on, babe. We gotta move."

Julie got the bench and stood up to release his right wrist, and then he held on with his right hand while she unhooked his left wrist. Bud dropped.

"Here, get these." Julie unsnapped his cuffs. "You get dressed. I'll see what they want."

Bud stood on his front porch in gym shorts and sandals, Elsie at his side. One word from him would launch her into attack mode.

The white Mercury parked behind Bud's wagon. Two men in white shirts with ties stayed in their car, the driver speaking from open window.

"Hello, are you Bud Richter?"

"Yes."

"Do you know Herbert Malik?"

"Yes."

Both men held up badges. "Mr. Richter, we're with the Federal Bureau of Investigation. We'd like to talk to you about Herbert, if we could."

"Come on up, fellas." He directed Elsie to the far end of the porch opposite the swinging bench, ordered her to stay there.

"John Petry." He shook Bud's hand with his right, presenting his badge for inspection with the left. "This here is Ray Mosier."

"Sorry to be such a slob. I was working out."

"Not to worry," said Petry.

"So, what's up with Herb?"

"That's what we'd like to know," said Mosier.

"Explain."

"Has he been here recently?"

"Sure was. A week ago... week ago today, I think. Said he's going to St. Louis to see his sister."

"He never arrived. Never came back to Denver, either."

"I'll be damned. Well, I'll tell you what I know. Would you like a drink? Hot or cold?"

"Some ice water sounds good," said Mosier.

"Would you like to do this inside or out?"

"It's a fine day, Mr. Richter..."

"Bud will do."

"Bud, let's stay out here," said Mosier, who took over the lead role between the two agents. Both men stood nearly six feet tall, Mosier in his forties, brown eyed and dark haired with greyed temples, Petry thirties, blue and brown. Both wore business suits sans jackets, Mosier navy, Petry tan. Their shirts were long-sleeved, sleeves buttoned, centered by diagonally striped neckties, knots loosened.

"Julie," Bud shouted through the front door screen. "Come out here a second."

Bud introduced her as his ex-wife, placed his drink orders including coffee for himself, and then told her to plan on joining them for a talk about Herb Malik.

"Let's go to the east side, fellas. In the shade." Here were two metal outdoor chairs and a small round table to match. Julie arrived with a tray carting four drinks, and after Bud took the tray and sat it on the table, he asked her to bring two kitchen chairs, while he introduced the men to Elsie. Bud's German Shepherd was acquainted with Agents Mosier and Petry in the same manner that she had met Herb, then ordered to sit at the other end of the porch near the swing.

With blue jeans, white sneakers and yellow t-shirt her attire, Julie set one chair at a time onto the porch and then joined her nearly-naked husband to converse with Agents Petry and Mosier. They sat circled around the table, the agents nearer the house and looking towards the yard. Mosier did most of the talking. Petry wrote notes onto a hand-held pad.

"Here's what we know, Bud... Mrs. Richter?"

"Julie," Bud answered.

"He left Denver about eight a.m. Monday morning. About what time did he arrive here?"

Bud looked to Julie, but answered for both. "Before noon. About eleven I'd say."

Petry jotted; Mosier talked. "Herbert's sister said he'd mentioned on the phone to her the night before that he'd be swinging through north Colorado to see an old Navy friend. Said he'd call her to confirm it, but that he planned to be at her place late Monday night. He never made the second call, and we've been unable to confirm that he was ever on I-70. That's the route he told her he'd take. Did you give him directions from here?"

"Yeah. In fact, I followed him to the 385... right over there." Bud turned and pointed to the distant junction. "Told him to turn left, south to I-70. I went right... north to Holyoke."

"Did he turn?"

"Yep. So did I. In fact, I watched in my rear view mirror until his car disappeared over the hill crest. Mercury... just like yours, except it was black. So, Herb never told his sister my name?"

"No. Took us awhile to figure out you might be that buddy of his. Had to go through Navy records and match names to known residences. Narrowed it down to you, a fellow in Fort Morgan and another in Julesburg.

"Don't know about the other two. He was here most of the day."

"Bud?" Julie tried to interject.

"Not now, honey," Bud stifled her. "He never mentioned the other two. Did he know them?"

"No. We've already spoken with them. They were from the Oriskany's roster."

"That's the carrier. We were on the cruiser together before he transferred."

"Bud?"

"What is it, Mrs... Julie?" Mosier wanted any and all information.

"Bud might strangle me for this, but he came back here that night."

"Who?"

"Bud came back here."

"Was that was the original plan?"

Bud fielded the question. "I drive for a truck line in Cheyenne. That's where I was headed, back to work, but after I saw Herb safely out of sight, I decided I had time to come back for a..." he looked at Julie. "Shall we say, quickie?"

"Yes, Agent Mosier," Julie confirmed. "That's exactly what it was."

"So, you and your ex-wife still... shall we say, do it?"

"Better than when we were married." He grabbed her hand. "And by the way. Look at me now. Just because I said I's working out doesn't necessarily mean weights."

"Sorry to interrupt."

"How could you know? Hey, that's why I came back here after Herb left. He'd kept us from doing our thing that day. Busy entertaining him."

"Had he been coming here on a regular basis?"

"No, no. I hadn't seen him since he transferred to the Oriskany. You know how it is. Fellas make promises to keep in touch, but rarely do. Hell, I thought he was still in New Jersey. Still called him Herbie when he got here, just like the old days. He got us to calling him Herb."

"Do you remember what time he left here Monday?"

"After dinner. Had to be around six-thirty, seven. I know the sun was a blinder on this road here. Smack dab in the center of the windshield."

"And he never mentioned stopping anywhere else? To visit anybody else?"

"No, sir. Said he was going direct to St. Louis. Julie would have let him stay the night that day he was here. We told him that, but he wanted to travel. I was hoping he might stop here again on the way back. He said he was going straight back to Denver after seeing his sister. That I should come and see him there if I wanted... told me that the highway goes both directions."

"Did he call you before coming here?"

"No."

"Mr. Mosier?" Julie asked permission.

"Yes, ma'am?"

"Herb stopped in Holyoke to ask about Bud. Our friend, Greg Dietrich called here for permission to give a man directions to our place."

"Who's Greg Dietrich?"

"He runs the Koffee Kup Kafe," Julie answered. "That's where Herb stopped to see if anybody knew Bud."

"Did you take the call, Julie?"

"Yes."

"Do you remember how much time elapsed between the phone call and Herbert's arrival here?"

"About thirty minutes. Right Bud?"

"Yeah, twenty to thirty... that's about right."

"Well, you've been very helpful. Both of you. Is there anything else you can remember that might be important?"

"I can't. Can you, Julie?"

"No. Not right now."

"We just talked, fellas. Julie fed him twice. We reminisced about the Navy and filled each other in on what's happened since. I gave him a little tour of the house, inside and out here. He said he works with you, right?"

"Yes. In another department, but we do know Herbert. Did he say anything that might have led you to believe there was anything wrong? Depression? Fear of anything?"

"Not at all. Said he was working on a case of mysterious skulls found around truck stops, but was on vacation for two weeks. I enjoyed seeing him, and I think he was comfortable here."

"Here's my card. If you think of anything else, don't hesitate to call us. Do you mind if I get your phone number here?"

"No problem. 524-5844."

"Would you gentlemen like another drink?" Julie asked.

"I don't. John?" He shook his head no. "We're fine. Thank you. I do need to use your rest room, if I may."

"Come with me." Julie escorted Mosier to the ground-floor bathroom off the former kitchen.

Bud Richter and John Petry endured an uncomfortable thirty-second silence, until Bud blurted a throwaway. "How do you like our muddy roads?"

"Farmers need the rain, I guess." Petry closed his notebook and laid it on the table. "This Iran thing's a real mess. Isn't it?"

"Yeah, well, that's what happens when you prop up a bad man. People in that country finally took charge. They hate us more than they hated the Shah."

"So, you're not angry about our hostages?"

"Ha. Never dreamed I'd be talking world affairs during this interview."

"Oh no, Bud. The interview's over. Just chit chat."

"It makes me sad, John, not angry. It's sad because we should have done it ourselves."

"What do you mean?"

"If we wanted to maintain our influence in that country, we should have replaced the Shah ourselves, rather than supporting him while he abused his people. How would you feel if say, the Soviet Union, chose our President and backed him up while he dismantled *our* Constitution, *our* rights and freedoms. How would you like it if your friends and family were put in prison for no good reason, tortured, killed, wouldn't it piss you off? Wouldn't you want to do something about it? Wouldn't you want to kill any Russian you could get your hands on? I know I would, so I understand why the Iranian people are doing what they're doing. It's our fault more than it is theirs. We played it wrong, and now we're paying for it."

"Bud, did you know Herbert is Pakistani?"

"Chit chat, huh? Is that what you called it?" Bud sat straight in his chair, hands firmly gripping its arms. He inflated his chest gorilla-like, menacing and threatening-like. Had he been duped? Yes, but just as with the Sacramento issue, Bud feared nothing. Agent Petry said nothing. Bud told the truth.

"Herb's parents are Pakistani, Mr. Petry. Herb Malik was born in New Jersey. That makes him an American, last I heard, right?"

"Yes, sir."

"Yes, sir," Bud mocked in repeating before continuing. "Herbie and I weren't just shipmates. We were best buds when we were on that ship. I don't see it. Ok? I don't give a shit. A man is straight up or he's counterfeit. That's all I see. So take your suggestion that I'm something I ain't and stick it up your ass."

"What's going on here?" Mosier returned with Julie close behind.

"Nothing, Agent Mosier. Everything is just frickin' fine and dandy."

"John?"

"I told Mr. Richter that Herbert's parents were from Pakistan."

"No, you didn't," Bud corrected. "You *asked* me if I knew *Herb* was Pakistani, which he is not."

"Agent Petry, to the car."

"I try to help you, answer your questions in good faith and have to put up with that bullshit."

"You're right, Bud. Agent Petry was out of line." The younger agent was halfway to the automobile, so Mosier spoke louder. "In fact. Agent Petry is an asshole. Please accept my apologies for leaving him alone with you."

"Agent Mosier, Herb is my friend. Seeing him again nearly brought tears, which ain't easy to do. Just ask my wife. I don't know what happened, but I sure as hell hope you can find him. I'll help you any way I can, but I'm only talking to you from now on."

"You've already helped a great deal. I'll be in touch. Let you know what we find out."

"Good, 'cause I wanna know."

Mosier shook hands with both Bud and Julie, thanked them, and headed for the car. Petry drove them away, neither man talking.

"Calm down, Bud."

He was standing in his posture of dominance, arms back, chest forward, breathing heavily and sweating again. "What time is it?" Bud asked, turning away from the view of auto leaving to the view of Julie concern.

"About thirty minutes before Lisa and Jack get here."

"Damn it to hell. What do you think?"

"I think you better shower, so you can visit with them not smelling like a horse."

"Hey, smell of a man, baby, and you love it."

"I suppose, sometimes. Right now I need you to smell like a civilized man, so get to it. I'll solve your problem when the time is right."

"Yes, ma'am. I'll do as you say."

"And don't forget to lock that door."

New Old Stuff

The plan was for Julie to fix dinner, while Bud spent time with Lisa and Jack, but that all changed with a phone call.

"Mom?"

"Hello, Lisa. Where are you?"

"At school. My car's a piece of crap. It just sits here... making noises."

"Hold on, Lisa. Your dad's here. Better tell him."

The gist of it was the engine wouldn't start, although it took Bud awhile to glean that information from his angry daughter. "I'll meet you at your car. Don't try to do anything with it. Leave it alone. Have you tried to call Jack's school?"

"No."

"Well, call over there and get a message for him to stay put. I'll pick him up."

"I'll have the office do it."

"Good. Give me half an hour." Bud came up behind Julie as she chopped vegetables at the counter. "The hell with you," preceded a kiss to the back of her neck. "My children need me."

"Let me know what's going on. Call me from somewhere."

"Yes, darling. You better call Jack's school and make sure he knows to wait for me, just in case Lisa, well, you know, doesn't."

Jack was waiting outside the front door of his school to join his father in riding to the high school. Other than teacher and administrator cars, the parking lot was mostly cleared out and Lisa's red Nova sat alone with Lisa inside.

Bud popped the hood. "Well, that was easy. Somebody pulled your spark plug cables. Wasn't that a hateful thing to do?"

"Idiots," Lisa snorted.

"Jack, you get that side."

"What am I doing?"

"What I'm doing. Lisa, have you been making the other girls jealous again?"

"Cute, dad. Ha, ha." Uninterested in the mechanics of the situation, Lisa sat in her driver's seat, fuming while waiting.

"Nothing to it, Jack. Just match 'em up where they're hanging.

This one goes to this plug. Yours goes there." Four on each side and all connections were reconnected. "Try it, Lisa."

The engine came to life and rumbled smoothly. "Jack, drop the hood." His downward push was weak, leaving the first catch engaged but the second one open. "Here, son." Bud released the latch and raised the hood. "Try it again."

He slammed it with all his might, successful, but frustrated with the entire ordeal. "I hate cars. Give me open air."

"Oh, yes. The motorcycle man. Are you riding with me or with her?"

Before Jack could answer, Lisa shifted to drive and slowly drove off, exiting the parking lot. "Does that answer your question, dad?"

"We men are just their slaves, Jack. Here to serve them."

Bud drove to Holyoke's downtown, passing by the Kup, where a white Mercury belonging to two FBI agents was parked. Passing by without turning his head, Bud continued to the next block, parking in front of Pete's Hardware and Auto Supply. "Wanna come in or wait here?"

"What are you doing?"

"Gonna fix Lisa's problem. Come on in with me."

Jack followed his father into the store, where owner Pete Lidell stood guard alone.

"Well, hello, Bud. How you been?"

"Better than worse, thanks. How about you, Pete?"

"Bored today. Guess everybody's broke after tax day. I sent Marvin home a couple of hours ago. Hey, is this your boy?"

"Sure is. Pete, this is my son, Jack Richter. Jack, this is Pete Lidell, owner and proprietor."

"Hi, Mr. Lidell."

"Hello, Jack. Haven't seen you since you were knee high to me."

"Jack's into motorcycles," Bud beamed. "Got him a motocross bike he rides all over hell and back."

"Never tried that. Kinda like to have steel around me."

"Not me, Mr. Lidell. There's nothing like the wind slapping your face, dirt flying off your wheels."

"Hey, you ought to see these new helmets we got." Pete headed down the aisle with Jack in tow, Bud trailing. "Latest design. Lightweight but solid."

Jack scrutinized the three choices, unimpressed. "Those look weird. Got any solid colors?"

"Nope, just these."

"Holy cow," Bud found one he liked. "This is the Captain America

128

helmet. From Easy Rider."

"What's that?"

"The movie."

"Never heard of it," Jack scoffed.

"Remember that, Pete?"

"Sure do. Great music. The ultimate biker's anthem. Born to be Wild."

"Try it on, Jack."

"Oh, dad, I don't like it."

"Then I will. Ouch. No, I won't... too small." Bud balanced the opening on top of his head and sang the song. "Get your motor runnin'."

The next line was Pete's. "Head out on the highway."

"Lookin'... lookin'..." Bud stared blankly. "Hell, Pete, I forgot the words."

"Yeah, me too."

It didn't matter. Jack had drifted away, landing amongst rows of men's work gloves.

"Give me this damned thing, Pete. If he won't use it, I'll just put it on a shelf and look at it."

Bud carried Captain America with him to join Jack. "Hey dad, I could use a pair of these black leather gloves for riding."

"Do they fit?"

He slipped his hand into the right one. "Yes."

"Bring 'em."

"What else, Bud?" Pete was enjoying this lucrative visit.

"I need hood locks for Lisa's automobile. Keep the riff-raff out."

To the automotive section they went, where Pete offered two types of kits. After carefully reading each box, Bud chose the higher-quality model even though it required more work to install. And since he was on a roll, Pete made one more suggestion.

"Hey, if you really want to keep the riff-raff out, look at this." Locked inside a glass casing along with mountable radios and tape decks, an alarm system. Pete opened the sliding door and brought it out. "Simple as can be. Mount it onto the bracket, run your wire to the steering column. This diagram shows you exactly which wires you splice it to."

"Then what?"

"Set this timer for when you leave your car. Set this one for entry. On switch. Off switch. That's it."

"Do you have to set the timers every time you wanna use it?"

"No. They'll stay the same until you change them."

"I assume it honks the horn."

"Yep, keeps blasting intermittent until you get in to turn off the alarm."

"Ah, I don't know, Pete. I've heard a gust of wind can set these things off. Lisa might get into trouble if her horn's going crazy all the time at school. Maybe I better not."

"Ok, Bud. Keep it in mind."

"I will, Pete. Guess that'll do it."

Jack had drifted away again, browsing Pete's limited supply of sports equipment. With money exchanged and items sacked, Bud was finished shopping.

"Jack, come on. Let's go home." He waited for his son to appear, and then turned to Pete. "Good seeing you."

"Same here, Bud. Thanks for coming in."

"I thought of you first."

"I know, Bud. It's been tough lately, so I really do appreciate it. Goodbye, Jack."

"Bye, Mr. Lidell."

Upon exiting, Bud glanced up the street to see the Mercury still parked in front of the Kup. Apparently Greg and Maggie had more to tell than Bud had figured on. Either that, or Agents Petry and Mosier had made a good choice for dinner.

"See how that worked, Jack?" Bud threw his bag into the back seat and started the wagon. "That's called service. Don't get that at these new, humongous super marts. That place is going to ruin the small businessman. Fellow like Pete doesn't have a chance."

"That place smells old."

"Just because it's old doesn't mean there's no value to it." The wagon turned south, heading home. "Some things need improving on, others don't. A place like Pete's means quality, even if it does smell funny."

"Like our house?"

"Yeah, like our house. Like your mom and me."

"I'd rather live in a new house. Why don't you just move us to Cheyenne with you?"

"Where would you ride your bike?"

"On the streets."

"Not until you're eighteen. It's illegal."

Jack couldn't argue that, but motorcycling was the furthest thing from his mind. "Dad, why can't we all be together? I don't like it when you're not there."

"Aw, Jack. Your mother and I, we... we just can't be together all the time. Do you remember how we used to argue? You were probably too little. Ask Lisa. She remembers. Your mom and I are much happier this way."

"But if you moved us to Cheyenne, at least we'd be where you are."

"But I'd be gone six days a week. What would be the difference? Don't I come home when I'm not on the road?"

"Yeah... usually."

"Then, what does it matter if you're here or in Cheyenne? Hell, you'd have to make new friends... new school... new everything. Lisa's only got one year after this one. She doesn't want to leave here, does she?"

"Don't know. Never asked her."

Bud turned onto Richter Road with the house in sight. Silence sounded better, and neither Bud nor Jack said any more until the muddy station wagon was parked. "Jack." Bud extended his arm atop the seat back, turning his body towards his son. "Are you really unhappy here?"

"I guess not. Just wish it didn't smell old."

"Your great, great grandfather and his brother built this house, Jack. Think about that. You like history. They were building this house about the time General Custer and his men were slaughtered by the Lakota Nation. We just saw the battlefield a couple of weeks ago. Can you picture it, Jack? Custer himself may have passed by here. Sitting Bull, Crazy Horse, may have taken shade beneath the very trees used to make the floors beneath your feet. Think on it, Jack. Imagine if the walls of this house could talk. It's a living museum, and it's yours, if you want it."

Jack sat staring past his father to the house beyond, its towering turrets, its ornamental metal roof, and he did think on it. He did imagine mighty warriors of the plains and their women and children moving in mass from a place of persecution, seeking safety until forced to migrate again. He pictured soldiers in blue, on horseback, long columns appearing on the crest of the hill, marching with purpose in pursuit of the heathens. And he understood what his father was talking about. Old meant quality. Old meant value. Old meant history worth keeping. Jack saw his old home in a new way, and he expressed it in a new way.

"This house rocks, dad."

"Like my Captain America helmet?"

"Ha... yeah, and your old rock and roll song."

"Music is like your house, Jack. Timeless. Either it's good or bad to begin with. It never changes. Come on before your mother skins us alive. Oh, my god... I was supposed to call her... we are in some serious trouble now."

All the after-dinner entertainment was Bud's idea. Whereas the normal routine would be Jack riding his motorcycle and Lisa telephone talking to friends in her room, Bud somehow convinced both that they might enjoy looking at pictures. In the downstairs northeast turret, the drawers of a wooden secretary belonging to Bud's paternal grandfather contained photo albums. This man died when Bud was three years old, but at age ten he had smartly, from curiosity, convinced the man's wife to write beneath each photo the names and relations of the people she knew and could remember. This came about because the woman grew weary of her grandson's incessant, "Who's that? And who's that?" questions with every photo viewed.

Bud removed these three photo albums and sat Julie, Lisa and Jack down on a comfortable couch, leaving them there to peruse the ancients while he worked in the garage. Holes were drilled into the hood of Lisa's auto, as Bud installed her new hood locks, following the written instructions word for word. After the mounting was completed, Bud tested the locks with the two keys provided, was satisfied with their functioning and pocketed both.

Since he was there, he raised the hood of Julie's 1977 Olds Cutlass, checked the oil which was dirty, and added radiator fluid to the proper level. After a stop in the bathroom to empty his bladder and wash his hands, Bud found the Richters right where he had left them, mother in the middle, children by her sides and each with their own opened photo album on lap.

They ignored him, and this pleased him. "Anybody I know?"

"Dad," Jack inquired. "I found a picture of your dad without his shirt. Wait... let me find it." He flipped a few pages. "Here."

Julie cringed, not knowing what a photograph of his father might do to Bud's good spirits.

"Well, let me see." Bud squeezed between Jack and the arm of the couch. "Yeah, that's him."

"How come you're all hairy and he isn't?"

"Oh, that's my mother's fault."

"What do you mean?"

"Her ancestors came from one of those Slovak countries. Romania? Let me think... ah, I can't remember. I'll have to ask her. Hell, I can't ask her. All she'll do is drool on me."

"Bud!" Julie scolded.

"No. I was the first hairy Richter we know of. Kinda makes you wonder how you'll turn out... eh, Jack?" Bud formed a fist and rubbed his boy's chest. "Don't worry, Jack. Better to have it than not. You can always shave it off if you don't like it."

"Every day?"

"Every day."

"You ever done that?"

"I don't think your mother'd like that."

"Bud, you didn't have a hair on you when we first met."

"Oh, yes I did, but not where you could see it."

"Dad! That's gross," Lisa finally expressed an opinion.

"Hey, Lisa, here is your key. Nobody can open your hood besides you... and me."

"How does it work?"

"You'll see 'em at the end of your hood above the bumper. Just like any other lock and key. There's two of 'em. Want me to show you?"

"No," she was insulted. "I think I know how to use a key."

"Well, thank god for that."

Lisa closed her photo album and set it onto the coffee table. "I'll see you guys tomorrow."

"No phone calls after eleven," her mother ordered.

"Ok, goodnight."

"Don't you have something to say to your father?"

"Thanks, dad," Lisa mono-toned.

"You're welcome, my sweet, precious, angel."

"Oh, brother."

"Guess I'll turn in, too." Jack set his book beside the first. "Thanks for letting us see the old pictures... and for my gloves." He started for the stairs.

"Hey, Jack. Story is that your great-grandfather was born in that room where you sleep."

"Really?"

"Yeah. Apparently in those days, the women just squatted like they were on the toilet and dropped their kids on the floor."

"Oh, Bud... really, that's enough." Julie properly feigned disgust, while Jack genuinely cracked up.

"Sure they did. That's a good one. Goodnight, everybody."

The two love birds were left alone on the couch, one quite proud of himself, the other very proud of him. Julie could not recall Bud ever reaching out for communication with Jack and Lisa before, at least not to this degree, and certainly not in regards to his family history. Perhaps his brush with death had elevated their value to him. Maybe both of his families, present and past were a bit more important than they were a week ago. She had no intention of analyzing or discussing the reasons for their perfect evening, but did intend to build on it.

Together they shut down the ground level of house, lights off, Elsie good nighted and doors locked. Julie led the way up staircase, where both Lisa and Jack occupied themselves in their rooms, doors closed with beams of light extending underneath.

"Goodni..." Julie's mouth was covered from behind by her husband's palm.

"They've said goodnight," he whispered. "Let 'em alone."

He guided her into their turret bedroom, closing the door behind them. They stood face to face, undressing, until Bud stood in boxers, Julie in panties. He waited for her. She completed her nakedness and he followed suit. All words were whispered, as they embraced breast to breast.

"Your skin... mmm... Julie, why do you feel so soft tonight?"

"Because I'm supposed to."

"Do I smell ok?"

"As long as you don't raise your arms." She separated from him, took his hand, led him onto the bed. She made him lay on his back atop the coverings. She pulled the pillows from underneath, tossed them to the floor and turned out the bedside table lamp. All went grey. "Raise your arms."

She took his right hand and guided it towards the bed post. He took hold. She circled the bed to do the same with his left hand, and then moved to the foot, grabbed his ankles and tugged, stretching him into a taut X. Crawling between his spread-apart legs, she hovered over him on all fours, her knees outside his hips. She lowered herself to lie with her breasts upon his chest, her belly above his belly, her vagina atop the base of his hardened shaft. She smothered his face with dry kisses. Her hands clutched his meaty forearms. She slimed his penis with woman juice, gliding ever closer to contact of long-suffering portal to ever-ready invader. And with connection made, she further lowered herself, reversing direction, caressing his penis with her velvety vaginal walls.

Julie Richter dominated her husband. He laid flat on his back, stretched and crushed beneath her weight, mesmerized, speechless and helpless to exert the energy required to lift her. She controlled the pace. She controlled the pressure, and Julie Richter was in no hurry to finish anything. She took him to deepest penetration, kept him there, squeezed him there, while forcing her hands beneath his back. She lifted his chest, flattened her breasts and stimulated herself with his friction, the friction of hard masculine skin and soft masculine fur. She shifted back and lifted his penis inside her, lifted his chest closer to her, and lost her face to the hair. She rubbed her cheeks on his sternum, on his pectorals. She engulfed his stretched tits with her mouth, sucked on the left one, and then the right, while absorbing the surrendered whimpers escaping his throat. She licked his arm pits, saturating them with spit, approving the smell of a man, the taste of a man -- her man.

Julie manipulated him, crushing him in the depths of her warm, wet vise. She removed her right hand from beneath his back, continued lifting him with her left. She leaned back until his penis was vertical, positioned her left hand to the small of his back and planted a right-hand claw to his belly. Her vaginal walls crushed him. Her penetrating fingertips impaled him, and she slowly, torturously raised herself to the top of his pole. Again she squeezed, brutalizing his corona, before gliding back down his shaft, her pace lingering, torturous.

She gave him warmth, she gave him wetness, but nothing more. Julie repeated her method of attack again and again, tormenting him from face to belly, never allowing his penis the friction necessary for his release. Bud was denied. He was denied his control, denied his masculine dominance, denied his orgasm. And with each passing minute, as the minutes became an hour, Bud was overwhelmed with desire for this woman. His bloodstream raged with testosterone. His emotions of manliness rose to a maddening height, until he begged for her to finish him, pleaded with her to allow his explosion, using no words of any language other than the language of sex. Bud's pitiful moans fell on deaf ears.

She journeyed with him to their beginning -- their second beginning, the night he showed up on her porch, his porch, the night of his confrontation with three men outside a Holyoke tavern. He appeared before her near midnight as a weathered alley cat, the hair on his head matted with dried sweat. His shirt waved in the breeze, overlapping his jeans, its buttons unbuttoned, most buttons missing. The matted hair of his chest and belly centered his opened shirt, splotches of red dotted his knuckles, the backs of his hands. He told her of his deed, of his manhandling of her husband, his pummeling of her husband's two friends, not knowing how she would respond, not knowing if she would be pleased or displeased. He surrendered to her, desperate for her acceptance.

She took his scarred hand, led him directly into the grey-shrouded turret, near this same bed in this same room. She stripped him of his tattered clothing, guided him to lay flat on her mattress, exhibited for him her newly-found skills, unknown even to her until executed. With her mouth she praised him, with her tongue she painted him, and with her throat she controlled him.

Bud had no choice but to reach for the bedposts. His reach was involuntary, but of his own doing. The overwhelming ecstasy of her touch stripped him of all misconceptions that he was the dominant partner. The power of her touch weakened him, sapped his strength, erased his ability to defy her. He stretched himself, demanding to be punished. Then as now, she punished him with denial. Their first session, a session of discovery, of secret desires learned in silence by movements and responses, sealed their reunion, rekindled their passion, while leaving their pain a distant memory. She controlled him, and with her domination she allowed him to exonerate himself from all guilt. With Julie in control, Bud's demons were extracted, taken from him, no longer his responsibility, no longer his problem. With Julie in control, Forrest Richter was dead, buried and forgotten.

Now as then, she became weary. She laid atop him where she had begun, keeping his penis imprisoned, crushed to the depths of her vaginal walls. Her head fell next to his, between his cheek and the crook of his shoulder. Her fingers encircled his triceps and biceps. Julie drifted into sleep.

It takes great strength for a man to lay flat on his back for hours, the weight of a woman bearing down on his chest, but Bud never wavered. All senses were focused upon the never-ending ecstasy of wet velvet surrounding his penis. Bud did not waver there, either. He could have released his hands and reasserted his dominance, but he never did. With his strength, he could have thrust his hips to finish himself from below, but no. Now as then, he needed her control and gladly accepted it. He waited for her while listening to her breath, wincing when her vaginal vise, either consciously or dreamily, squeezed the thickness of his erection. He left her undisturbed, and waited for her to decide.

In time, perhaps an hour perhaps two, Julie was elevated to that lingering state between dream and reality, and she brought Bud's corona to her clitoris. She targeted herself, methodically and slowly clipping her trigger against the rim of his mushroom, until she was fully awakened and raised to sit vertically atop him. She bounced him, pressing fists into his belly for leverage. She did the work, and her howls of pleasure could not be suppressed, nor could his. And when both man and woman had combined their fluids and returned from the dizzying heights of their self-imposed, pressure building session of denial, Julie ordered him off the bed, turned down the covers, replaced the pillows and slept in front of him. Laying on their sides, they spooned, his manly breath warming her neck, his muscular arm wrapped around her rib cage, his scratchy fingertips massaging her nipples.

It takes great stamina for a woman to withstand the power of a man's penis for hour after hour. Julie's gait was altered next morning. Savvy-teenager Lisa knew why, but said nothing. Quickly-learning Jack suspected, but never questioned. He hoped that the sounds he'd heard were of pleasure, not pain. For Lisa, there was no doubt. She remembered from her childhood their sounds of pain, of arguments, of shouting matches and tears. The sounds coming most recently from their room were far preferable, and even though the image of her parents doing it was "gross," as Lisa would put it, the knowing that they did it more often now than ever before was "way cool."

Bud and Julie saw their kids off to school, Bud showing Lisa how to use her hood locks despite her protests. They stood on the front porch until the red Nova turned onto the 385.

"Are you hungry, Bud?"

"For what?"

Old lovers, old discoveries made new, in an old house with old smells, Bud and Julie wasted their morning by smelling, touching and tasting one another. No penetration necessary, only mouths and tongues, with no words spoken.

Loose Lips

Bud was expecting any one of a number of telephone calls, but the one of which he was most certain came Tuesday afternoon.

"Bud, it's Perry. The funeral is tomorrow."

"Where?"

"Laramie. Parker Memorial Chapel."

"When?"

"One o'clock."

"I'll stay here tonight. Be in Cheyenne about nine-thirty or ten. Are we taking a crew from Pearsall?"

"I'm going. Jenny's riding with me. That's all I know so far."

"I'll ride with you, if that's ok. Be at your office by eleven."

"Good enough, Bud. See you then."

A funeral was never mentioned to Julie. Bud's leaving early was for the Freightliner investigation, nothing more. In time he would tell her of Harry's demise, but for now the connection of two faulty tractors, one dead driver and one could have been dead driver would be for Bud to know and for Julie to never suspect.

He was surprised to see Jack wearing the Captain America helmet for his after-dinner motorcycle ride. Jack summoning his sister and asking his father to explain more of the pictures to them pleased Bud even more. They sat at the rarely-used dining table in the downstairs northwest turret, father flanked by children. Losing interest after an hour, Lisa expressed her thanks and went upstairs to use her phone until bedtime. As for Jack, he found interest in pictures of his great-grandfather posing both inside and outside the barn he'd built.

"Has it always been white?"

"No, Jack. I remember it being a dark red. I think that was its original color."

"Why don't we paint it red again?"

"We?"

"Yeah, why not?"

"You gonna climb a ladder up there? I'm not sure I'd want to."

"I'd do it."

"I think you might want to stand next to it and look up before you make any commitments."

"The inside was pretty fancy, huh?"

"Oh, sure. Used to have cattle running in and out. Even had several milk cows at one time. That's what these stalls were for."

"Everything's broken in there now."

"It's old and tired."

"I wanna make it old and strong again."

Bud leaned back in his chair to ponder this. The time involved, money spent, and worst of all, labor expounded all combined to make the granting of Jack's wish a daunting task. But it could be done, with a little coordination, planning and help of friends.

"Why don't you do this, Jack? Draw me up some ideas for the inside, you know, like maybe a storage and maintenance area for your bike, and when I get back next time I'll talk to Wilton and Mark. Wilton's got one of those trucks with a lift. If I can get them on board, if we can work out a money agreement, then that will be our summer project. Ok?"

"A lot of 'ifs'."

"That's the way it goes. Life is full of 'em."

Jack was satisfied, and they found more pictures featuring the barn, several with Bud's father. He got through them unscathed, grateful that Jack asked very little about him, figuring that at some time or another Julie had made it known to Jack that the subject of his grandfather Forrest was a touchy one for Bud.

Once Bud left his house on Wednesday morning, after seeing the kids off to school, he drove non-stop to Cheyenne. His nursing home visit would have to wait until after Mother's Day. First stop, his apartment to don one of the two suits he owned - black for funerals; grey pinstripe for weddings.

The Pearsall contingent was three: Perry drove, Jenny in front, Bud in back. Recorded organ music was playing in the chapel when they arrived for Harry's closed-casket memorial. Harry's wife was there, whom Bud had met. Harry's two grown kids were there. Harry was preceded in death by his parents, survived by two sisters. They were there and they had assisted his wife with the arrangements. Together, the Pearsall three introduced themselves and expressed sorrow to family, at which time Harry's wife asked if one of Harry's co-workers could speak of him during the service. The nominee was Bud. He agreed to this, and asked permission for the director to play a song from his tape. Permission was granted without questions.

The service started with a vocalized recording of Amazing Grace. *Surprise!*

A preacher of limited speaking abilities was in charge of eulogizing

Harry Preston. Wearing a cheap grey suit, the man appeared past retirement age and probably performed such services for extra cash. He began by forcing all in attendance to listen to his short prayer, and then announced the reason for the gathering, to remember and celebrate the life of Harry Preston. He'd never had the privilege of meeting Harry Preston, this he admitted, but he knew Harry as a brother in Christ, one of god's children. He held up a newspaper clipping, the obituary, and read it word for word. It's print too small for him to see, he brought the paper directly in front of his eyes, covering his face as he spoke, but still he repeatedly stumbled, stuttered and mispronounced words.

He opened the Bible and read some Old Testament passage, something he should have known by memory had he prepared himself properly, but even this was mangled. Despite the bad beginning, things only got worse for the imprisoned victims forced to listen, as the preacher launched into a lengthy, condescending and threatening diatribe about what you can and cannot do if you want to go to heaven. None of it pertained to Harry, other than the theory that had Harry known of the wonderful world awaiting him he might have done this or he might not have done that.

Bud was fidgety. He crossed his legs. He uncrossed them. He looked at his watch. He folded and unfolded his arms, shifted his butt from left to right, and sighed heavily and loudly and frequently.

The man's speech droned on for more than thirty minutes, deteriorating to a rant of his own self-loathing, of how he used to drink and fight and beat his wife and whip his children, until Jesus came into his life and made him whole.

By the time this man had finished tormenting his audience, Bud was agitated, Jenny exhausted and Perry worried. As the preacher sat, music began. It was a song from Bud's tape, given to him by Jimmy the morning Bud started out in one of two doomed Freightliners. The musicians? Jimmy Martin and the Sunny Mountain Boys, and their song title, *Widow Maker*.

As the a capella harmonies sang the introduction, Bud rose and moved to the podium. A banjo was the first instrument heard, and Jimmy Martin sang the first verse of this trucker's tale, of a driver who takes his rig off the road to avoid plowing into a stalled pick-up filled with children. The smiles staring back at Bud told him that all were relieved to know Harry's genuine eulogy was finally underway.

"That song right there sums up the Harry I know," Bud began at music's end. "I don't know that he ever beat his wife or his kids. If he did I never heard about it."

Bud looked at the preacher, who sat with a dull glow of piety as though he didn't know the barb was aimed at him. Perhaps he didn't.

"As for drinking, well, he's always under control with that, and what a man does on his own time is his business. I never, ever saw him hit a man who didn't deserve it. It's like the fastest gun in the west. Every young punk wants to challenge him. Harry's always being challenged. Harry scares people, but it's not his fault. He's built big, strong, intimidating, but inside he's a softie, a kind-hearted soul to people who are kind to him. Harry's been my friend for nine years and I've enjoyed every minute of it. He's an A-One professional truck driver and he is proud that he never once has had an accident, or gotten any tickets from the law. His first accident will be his last, and it's no accident that he sacrificed himself to save others. That's the Harry I know. That's the Harry we all know."

Bud returned to his seat and the preacher moved to the podium for a closing (everybody hoped) prayer, but one of Harry's sisters stood and thanked everyone for coming. She waved to the funeral director, who came down the aisle and announced the place of burial. The procession would depart in fifteen minutes, after the family spent time with their loved one.

Harry's sisters managed to stifle the preacher there, too. Perry said a few words, as did Harry's wife and children, and then they dropped him into the ground.

And so, the long session of goodbye ended with everyone satisfied, except that Bud forgot to get his tape from the funeral director. No matter. He'd be passing through Laramie countless more times. Bud was now Pearsall's senior driver.

It was fitting that the three Pearsall employees would return to find things rather quiet in their terminal building. A somber atmosphere on a somber day, the only activity on the docks was the foreman taking inventory, the part time dispatcher filling in for Jenny, and Robert Carlyle struggling on his second day at a new position. The foreman had assigned him the duty of breaking down a trailer and he was making a mess of it.

"Hey, Robert. How's it going?"

"Hello, Mr. Richter. I'm getting the hang of it... I think."

Boxes all of shapes and sizes were stacked willy-nilly just inside the dock bay, some nearly blocking the path of boxes still needing to come in from the trailer. Robert was little by little boxing himself in.

"Looks like you're headed for disaster, buddy. What's on this trailer?"

"Uh... not sure."

"Has anybody explained to you what the hell is going on?"

"Not really, other than to stack 'em onto my two wheeler and get 'em on the dock. I'm supposed to distribute them to other bays, but not quite sure which ones, yet."

Bud wasn't surprised by any of this. Casting new employees into hopeless situations is a common procedure by many dock foremen. It's their way of testing a man's meddle, to see if he's smart enough and tough enough to find the answers and see the job through, and the three to eleven shift was the perfect training ground because rarely was there any great rush to get anything done.

"Well, Robert, let me explain a little bit to get you started." Bud took off his jacket and hung it on the handle of an idle two-wheeler. "First things first, let's look at your invoice." Robert retrieved it and handed it to Bud. "Ok, look right here. This trailer came from the John Deere warehouse in Cheyenne. See that?"

"Yes."

"Ok. Now look at this list. Everything is packed in lots according to destination. Page after page. See?"

"Yes, sir."

"Ok. All those docks on that side of the building are for outgoing freight. Each bay has a list of cities where that driver is going to go with the trailer from that bay. You will get to the point where you have most of them memorized, but as for now, you'll have to go look at the lists. I can tell you, for example, that Bays One and Two are for Cheyenne and Laramie. You will use those a lot. The containers on your trailer are going out tomorrow on twenty-seven-foot trailers or on straight trucks. Day trips, daily routes. So, your best bet is to look at your labels, stack a group with the same destination onto your dolly, take 'em over to that side and then find the bay for that town. If you try to sort 'em out over here you're gonna get jammed up. See?"

"I think so."

"Here. Fill up my dolly and then you can follow me with yours. Bring your invoice with you. We'll distribute them when we get over there."

Once on the outgoing side of the terminal docks, Bud took Robert on a walking tour of each bay to look at the city lists, and then had him distribute the freight they had brought over.

"You'll get yourself a system going before long. If you see on your invoice a large number for one city, stack 'em on a flat cart. Saves you steps."

Bud stood by while Robert distributed what they had two-wheeled over, and then cut him loose. "I'll leave it with you. That'll give you an idea as to what you're doing and why."

"Thanks, Mr. Richter."

"You're welcome. I'm pretty sure I told you to call me Bud."

"You did. Thanks, Bud."

"Ok. Better run. Funerals wear me out."

"That sure was sad, about that driver."

"No doubt. Harry was a good man. Did you get to meet him?"

"No. My first day of training Wally said something about him and you being the hot shots getting new tractors. Of course, I didn't know who or what he was talking about. He'd been out there looking at the... what were they... Kenworths?"

"Freightliners."

"Yeah, he said they were real beauties."

"Beautiful killers." An image of Harry desperately fighting to save his rig flashed by, but Bud instantly nixed that thought. "Well, at least you got to meet me. New tractor couldn't kill me, but it sure tried."

"Glad you made it back."

"Me, too. See you, Robert."

Bud carried his jacket with him in seeking out the dock foreman, informing the man that he'd given the new guy a couple of pointers. He grunted, expressed displeasure.

"Should have asked me first, Richter."

"Yeah, but you would have told me no. I just got him started. Trying to give him a chance to figure it out on his own."

"He'll never last."

"Maybe, but at least now it'll be because he can't take the physical part of it. He's got the brains to be a good worker, once he gets toughened up."

"We'll see." With another grunt of skepticism, the foreman went back to taking his inventory.

Bud stopped at Bud's Diner for an early evening meal before heading to his apartment, where he hung up his suit and collapsed in his recliner naked but for his underwear and socks. He dozed off and on, remembering Harry and their many shared bar room exploits. Fights? Sure, but the better memories were of conversations. Harry as mentor, that's what Bud would cherish, the trick of juggling life on the road with the needs of a wife and kids. Bud was still learning, still growing in this never-ending battle, but Harry had steered him the right direction. Bud figured Harry would continue to teach him. He felt confident that Harry would join the ranks of Bud's other-worldly protectors. Bud also knew that despite all attempts by the preacher to spoil it, Harry would appreciate the final farewell he received. Bud and Harry would forever be friends, and for this Bud was grateful.

Sand and Blood

No alarm clock was set. Bud slept in, awakened near noon by a ringing telephone. It was Jenny with his itinerary, a luxury bestowed but to him and Harry. The other drivers had to get theirs from her at her desk, and Bud was glad to know that Jenny had not demoted him to their rank, despite whatever the hell he'd done to sour her attitude towards him.

"You'll leave here tonight at seven for St. Charles, Missouri."

"That's north of St. Louis."

"Thank you, mister know-it-all. Pick up in the morning in Granite City, Illinois. Do you know how to cross the Mississippi River?"

"Touche, baby cakes."

"From there to..."

So began a circle of cities as far east as Pittsburgh and as far north as Chicago. Six days on the road were laid out in audio, so Bud could plan for what he'd see later in detail on printed page. He made himself some coffee and a sandwich comprised of Julie roast beef, then packed for his trip. The duffel given to him by Julie in 1963 wasn't big enough, and since the police still had his road duffel, Bud packed a hard-cover suitcase for clothes and his Julie duffel for in-the-cab needs.

He shit, showered and shaved, stopped again at his favorite diner, and appeared inside the terminal office at three-fifty-five, where one Freightliner representative conversed with Perry while waiting for Bud.

"Donald Ferguson."

"Bud Richter," he offered his hand.

"You did one heck of a job saving our tractor."

"Have you seen it?"

"Yes. I was in Salt Lake when I heard about the other one. I've seen it, too, or what's left of it."

"Bud," Perry wedged in. "Let's go to my office." The two sat in front of Perry's desk as he closed the door. "Mr. Ferguson, he's all yours."

"I'll want you to describe how the unit reacted to your attempts to control it after losing the transmission, but that can wait. Something else has come up."

"What?"

"Your transmission had sand in the fluid." Bud's eyebrows curled, mouth twisted. "Sand?"

"Yes. Somewhere between our final inspection before delivery here and the time you departed, someone dropped sand into the openings where fluid is added."

"Openings? You mean both tractors had it?"

"Yes. We grounded all those models all over the world and had them inspected. Only yours and Mr. Preston's had sand in the transmission."

"Holy shit, Perry. What's going on?"

"Good question. I've made a list of our employees who had access to those units before you guys drove them out. Clyde Overton did our inspections that morning and passed them. Here's his work order, signed two-fifty-seven a.m. for Harry's, four-forty-two for yours. Jimmy hostlered both of them onto your trailers. Here's his paperwork. Six-eleven for Harry's, Six-fifty-three for yours. Who else would have been around them?"

"Don't know. Where were they parked?"

"Clyde put them in B-6 and 7."

Bud executed his finger-through-hair brain stimulation... thinking... only two other men would have had access to the lot during those times, one who might have cause and one who might have some useful information.

"Fellas, wait right here," Bud piped. "I've got an idea that's making me sick to my stomach."

He went to the docks, where Robert was breaking down a trailer with a bit more organization than the previous day.

"Hi, Robert."

"Hello, Bud. Think I'm getting the hang of it, but I'm sore as can be."

"Oh, that's one thing you can count on. You will be a hard body in no time. Just gotta work through it for the first few days."

"That's what I'm trying to do."

"Right now you can take a little break and come with me."

"What's up?"

"We're having a little discussion in Mr. Jacobs's office and need you to join us."

Robert kept pace with Bud, and after his introduction to the Freightliner man, Robert was queried about his first day on the job, and Bud did the asking.

"Do you remember what time you started?"

"Five o'clock."

"And what happened first?"

"Well, Wally gave me a bunch of paperwork to fill out... you know, insurance applications and stuff. Then he gave me an employee's manual and told me to read it until he got back."

"And when he got back, is that when he made his comment about the new trucks?"

"Yeah."

"What did he say?" Perry wanted to know.

Robert had a decision to make. Was somebody in trouble? Was he going to be looked upon as a back-stabber. Two-faced? He needed Bud for reassurance.

"Don't you worry, Robert. You're with me, now. I ain't gonna let anybody hurt you. Neither is Mr. Jacobs. Tell it like it happened."

"He said that Harry and Bud were the hot shot drivers getting those new tractors. Talked about how beautiful they were."

Perry looked at Bud before asking his next question. "Is that all he said about that?"

"Yes, sir."

"Do you remember about how long he left you alone with your paperwork?"

"Thirty minutes... maybe forty-five."

"What did you do after that?"

"Nothing. He showed me the forms for doing inspections, and then I followed him every time a truck came in or out. Watched him do the work, until my shift was over. Next day he let me do it and he watched."

"Did you ever smell alcohol when you were around him?" Perry wondered.

"No, sir. Never did."

"Ok, thank you, Robert. How do you like the docks?"

"Hard work, but Mr. Richter, Bud, he showed me some tricks yesterday, so I think I'm getting it figured out."

"Good. You'll get a system going before long. Better get back to it."

Before Robert could get out of the office, Bud landed a soft fist to his shoulder. "Thanks, pal. Everything you heard and said stays right here in this office. Ok?"

"Sure, Bud."

"I'll look you up before I pull out of here."

As the door closed, Perry looked to Bud. "What do you think?"

"I think it's possible. I tell you one thing, that kid is honest." Bud explained how Robert refused to leave the Jeep idling the night they met, of how Robert turned off the engine even though Bud had told him he didn't need to do so.

"Ok, Bud. I know you know." Next, Perry needed Bud's take on the ex-truck driver. "What about Wally?"

"You know Wally. He's a great guy until he takes a drink. You wanna know what Wally thinks? Take him to a tavern. Get a couple of shots in him and bring up the subject of Harry. See what happens. I'd do it myself, but might kill him if he said the wrong thing. Besides, you're sending me to god knows where."

"And I can't afford to keep you here, either. We're a driver short."

"A good driver short." Bud cast his eyes to the floor, not sad, but seething, face red.

"Right," Perry agreed. "We lost our senior man over this, Mr. Ferguson, so we want to get to the bottom of it as badly as you do. What's the latest word from your insurance company?"

"Oh, they are very much involved. Got their own investigation going."

"Well, get them set up to see me. Maybe we'll just have a little chat with our gate attendant."

"I'll have them here tomorrow. Give me a time."

"After lunch. Two p.m."

Ferguson then pulled out a clipboard and paper form from his briefcase. "Mr. Richter, can you tell me how the unit responded? What you did to control it, and such?"

"Oh, you mean..." Bud snapped out of his growing hatred of Wally, took a deep breath and gathered his thoughts. "I didn't think you'd need to know. Someone put sand in your transmission, for Christ sakes. Are you gonna design a truck that can deal with it?"

"I need my report. Sorry."

Perry sat back to enjoy the coming entertainment.

"Ok, Mr. Ferguson. I can't tell you any more than the skid marks and police report already told you. It seemed a little rough going through the Three Sisters, but it was minor. Since it was new, I thought nothing of it. Never did much shifting again until heading into Salt Lake. I take it out of gear and it locked me out... neutral all the way. Just the grind of death... that's all I could get out of it."

"What was the sound it made?"

"Well, shit... like the sound it would make if you tried a gear with the clutch out. You know, like the teeth were biting to keep me out instead of letting me in."

"And then?"

"Oh, you want the rest? What the hell. From then on, a man doesn't think, he just does. I tried to save the brakes as much as I could. Kept double clutching trying to catch a gear. I'm on a six degree grade for god knows how many miles, picking up speed, praying the cars get out of my way and that the runaway ramp gets there before I'm going too fast to take her in there. Once I did get the ramp I suppose I breathed a little easier, I don't know. At least I wasn't gonna take anyone else out with me. It was just me and her and I figured we were gonna crash right through that barrier. I'm sure my speed dropped when the pavement leveled out. Never looked. Felt like I was slowing, but not enough. Kept pumping the brakes, popping the clutch and trying any and every gear. I was outta time. Gonna have to lock her up and see where the skid took me, but a split second before doing that, I caught a gear. A low one. Teeth were flying, the entire front end grinding, and the damned thing stopped. The beautiful son of a bitch stopped in a line as straight as a hard dick, me, my trailer, and your Freightliner. Why did I make it and Harry didn't? I was going downgrade. He was going up. And yet, here I am and he's dead. What does it mean? Either your time's up or it ain't. It's got nothing to do with driving ability. A man reacts, plays his cards best he can and hopes he comes out a winner. That's all it is. Did you get all of that?"

Of course, he didn't. Bud was talking a mile a minute. Mr. Ferguson would need to rely on his memory to file his report, a job made more difficult when Bud added a follow-up.

"I don't mean to be hateful, but I'm looking at a three-thousand mile trip in about two hours. It takes a certain mind-set to deal with that, and this right here is not helping me any. This will be my first out since what happened happened. I've lost a good friend, and I'm trying my best not to go find the bastard who did it and beat him to a bloody pulp. So, I hope you'll understand that right now I need to get the hell out of here and get my mind straight. Ok?"

Perry didn't stop him. Neither did the Freightliner man. Bud headed for his Custom Cruiser wagon for some solitude, but feared he might start the engine and drive somewhere in a fit of rage. He turned towards the break room, but was fearful of whom he might see in there. Any wrong word could be disastrous for any person within his reach. He turned another direction, nearly in a trance, not planning or even realizing where his steps were taking him. Bud walked right past Robert, who had his back turned looking at labels. He entered the trailer the young man was breaking down. Bud followed an open path made from Robert's work. The path took him nearly to the front of the trailer. With a maddened strength, he moved by hand three stacked boxes to make himself a cubby hole, and Bud Richter fell to his knees in despair.

No man can predict his response to grief. There are no schedules for when a breakdown should occur, or if one should occur at all. Bud's grief was not only for Harry, but for the culmination of events -- from his own brush with death to the battles with his wife to the battles with Harold Turley to the horrors of war to the tragedies of his childhood, and they all crashed upon him at once, as though a scorned woman whacking him with a cast iron frying pan. He cried no tears. All release was vocal. He clutched his head with his hands, staring at the grey metal of darkened trailer floor, and he whimpered. Each breath brought increased volume, until he moaned, and then he howled with a blood-curdling wail to awaken the dead, pleading with the powers that be to explain their reasons. Why, oh god, why did they keep him here to suffer? What more did they want from him? What was it they wanted him to do? Self-pity, self-loathing, all dark emotions that should be eliminated but instead are suppressed, could not be suppressed, for this is grief, and when it comes there is no stopping it. This is what the gods want from us. They bring forth these thoughts to remind us that we still have work to do.

"Bud? Mr. Richter?" Only Robert had heard Bud's sorrow. He had allowed Bud several minutes alone after realizing who was in his trailer, not because he recognized that Bud needed solitude, but because he was afraid to approach a stricken man. Bud knew Robert was there, but did not answer. Grief was subsiding, reversing its presence from wails to moans to whimpers, until Bud was ready to once again face another human.

"Yeah... hi, Robert." Bud slowly rose to his feet, made sure he had regained control of himself, and turned around. "Kinda had a little melt down there... hit me all at once... Harry and all... you know."

"Makes sense."

"Sorry I chose your trailer... you know... for my fit."

"No problem. Thought I'd let you know that I was gonna quit yesterday, until you came along to help me. I've changed my mind... you changed my mind."

"Good for you, Robert." Bud's good-natured self was resurrected. "You made a smart decision. Tell you something else, too. You got in good with the boss today. You keep working hard and stay on his good side. He'll take care of you. Ok?"

"I sure will."

"Ok. Time for me to get myself ready for pulling out of here. See you in about six days, if you're on the clock."

"Have a safe trip, Bud."

Bud was ready. All the clutter had been released. Robert was his new friend, someone he could mentor the way Harry had done him. Bud stopped at the dispatcher desk to get his paperwork and log book from Martina. His trailer was in outgoing Bay 7. He hostlered his tractor himself. He'd told Jimmy he wanted Matilda back and she was serviced, inspected, washed and waiting, documents proving it on her driver's seat. He got her from the lot and backed her into his trailer, raised its legs, hooked up hoses and wires, and pulled away from the dock. Parked, he did a walk around, closing and locking the trailer doors, inspecting wheels and lights. He walked to his car, got his two bags and threw them into Matilda along with his papers and log book. His traditional break room routine was completed at six-fifty-three. Bud and his rig sat at the outgoing inspection gate at seven p.m. A new man, freshly trained and released for solitary duty by Wally, gave Bud the ok to begin his journey.

Maggie Pie

Long-distance Suffering

The road gave Bud no headaches. He felt comfortable to be back in his Kenworth, along with its eight-track tape deck playing his familiar, duffel-bagged selections of music. Bud traveled the I-80 through Nebraska, stopping in Omaha for a meal and leg stretch, but rather than continue through Iowa where he'd pass by the scene of Harry's wreck, he cut south into Missouri on I-29 through Kansas City, where he connected to I-70 east to St. Louis. Delivery made, he crossed the Mississippi River into Granite City, Illinois on I-270. To his right stood the old, two-lane steel truss Chain of Rocks Bridge, what was the Route 66 crossing, now abandoned except for those who live there watching over Bud and his kin.

After pick up he reconnected with I-70, stopping at a rest area for a one-hour nap before continuing to Effingham. Arriving past the Friday noon hour, Bud checked into a truck stop motel room for serious sleep, calling to check up on Julie and the kids first.

"Bud, Lisa just called. She went to her car during her lunch break and all four tires were flat."

"What? How? They been cut?"

"I don't know. She just said they were all four out of air."

"Well, call Pete Lidell. Have him send his man over there. If they're not cut, he'll put air in 'em. If they are, tell Pete to replace the tires."

"Wait, Bud. I can't remember all this." She wrote down what he'd told her. "Ok, what else?"

"Tell Pete I want Goodyears. And tell him I want that alarm system he showed me the other day. Tell him to do what needs to be done and we'll settle up when I get back."

"Bud, I've got the money. We've got more than enough in my account."

"Whatever. Just call Pete and let him handle it."

What began as a routine, trouble-free road trip gradually deteriorated into a stressful nightmare. Bud was worried. The prank of pulling spark plug wires was just that, a prank, or so he thought at the time, but a second prank of letting air out of all four tires was no laughing matter. Cutting tires could only be considered a threat. He tried to sleep, but for once his internal clock would not obey his command. Curiosity ate him alive. It festered with each passing minute, and so he dressed and walked to the restaurant, found a booth with a phone and called again while waiting for his food to arrive.

"Is Pete on it?"

"He said he'd send a man to fix it."

"Have you talked to him again?"

"He said the tires were cut. He's replacing them."

"You need to go to the school." He looked at his watch. "It's three o'clock. I want you to go get Jack, then Lisa. Call Pete and tell him to have his man drive Lisa's car out to the house and you'll take him back. I don't want her driving that car. I want my kids home and I want them to stay there. Do you understand?"

"Yes, Bud. Where are you?"

"Illinois."

"When are you coming back?"

"I'm staying the night here, then Pittsburgh. Chicago by Monday and back on Wednesday, Tuesday late if I push it."

"Wish you could come home."

"Me too, but you know I can't. Listen, keep them home over the weekend. I don't want them going anywhere with anybody. And you pay close attention to Elsie. If she barks once, you find out why. Ok?"

"I will... And Bud?"

"Yes, Julie."

"That Agent Mosier called. They found Herb's car in the South Platte."

"In the river? Oh, shit. Where?"

"North of Sterling."

"That's about fifty miles. Was he in it?"

"No."

"Not in the direction of I-70, is it?"

"Certainly not."

"Don't like the sound of that. Let's hope there's a good reason and a good end."

"I love you, Bud."

"I love you, too. Don't be saying that. We're too far apart. And don't forget to keep them in that house. In fact, call Wilton and tell him what's going on. He'll keep an eye on you."

"Ok, Bud."

"You better go. School's gonna be out soon."

After his meal, Bud felt a little more content that he had done all he could from long distance. His over-extended body forced his brain to shut down. Bud slept hard and deep, awakening refreshed from a healthy

154

seven hours. Another call told him that all was normal in Holyoke. The Chalmers family had joined Julie and the kids for dinner. Wilton's children were spending the night, and their father would be back to check on them before bed time and again at sunup. Not a sound had come from Elsie, other than the friendly barks upon the Chalmers's arrival.

Bud crossed from Illinois into Indiana free of worries. The night sky was clear, air crisp and moon shining brightly. He could once again concentrate on what lay ahead and not what was happening fifteen hundred miles behind.

Clouds had formed to mask the sunrise. Outside of Columbus, Ohio, he stopped for a meal and a phone call. Greg Dietrich was in the Julesburg hospital. He had been severely beaten sometime and somewhere after closing the Kup on Friday night. Bud told Julie that his kids were *not* going to school Monday. They were *not* to leave the house for any reason whatsoever. No motorcycle, no automobile, no nothing.

From Pittsburgh he learned that Herb Malik had been found about forty miles east of Sterling, beaten, bound, buried and dead.

Outside of Chicago came news that Greg Dietrich had slipped into a coma, his chances of recovery diminished. Mark was with his mother at Greg's bedside, and so was unharmed when his house was set afire on Sunday. Bud told Julie to get his pistol from the basement file cabinet. She had never used it. Didn't know how, but only she and Bud were aware of that.

With his mid-morning pick-up in Wheaton, Illinois on Monday, Bud began the longest journey of his life. Nine hundred miles of pure hell that seemed to never end. For every hundred that should have passed, a mere twenty was the reality. He stopped looking at Matilda's odometer. Each reading only depressed him, distressed him further.

His last conversation with Julie had been ugly. She did not want the pistol in her children's presence. She wanted their father home. She wanted him to call Perry Jacobs and tell him to replace Bud with another man to finish the run. She wanted the impossible, the illogical, and their argument harkened back to days of old -- a battle of wits between an hysterical woman and a man full of rage. Bud was helpless, isolated, and in danger of breaking his own rules. Bud was tempted to push himself too far, tempted to keep himself awake by use of pills, tempted to deny his body nourishment and rest.

Bud Richter did not succumb to these temptations. An exit outside of Des Moines, six hundred miles from his home base reminded him that he was a professional. Bud took this exit, up the same ramp Harry had taken. Below him and to his left he saw the scars, paint of white and blue upon the scraped concrete of support column. He was traveling I-80, but on a bypass built to skirt the city. Route 30, the old Lincoln Highway, was several miles to the south, but that was fine because Harry wasn't there. He was here. Harry manned this post.

Bud parked his rig where Harry had intended to go. He filled his belly, checked into a motel room and slept undisturbed. He would be one hundred percent alert for his final push. Whatever troubles awaited would have to wait without him. The job came first. Without the job his family would starve. So what good would it do to risk the job in order to save the family? Harry's mantra came through loud and clear, and the I-80 from Des Moines to Cheyenne was a complete reversal from the Chicago to Des Moines leg. These miles disappeared. What seemed like one hundred was two. Without planning and without effort, Bud arrived in Cheyenne before the sun set on Tuesday. Wally was in prison. Bud didn't care. Perry told Bud Richter to go home -- his family home.

Hayseeds

No need to bother with local law enforcement. Even though it was obvious as to whom was responsible for the beating of Greg Dietrich and the torching of his son's house, the current sheriff couldn't figure it out if he tried, which he wouldn't.

No time for mushy, drawn-out hello's either, but that didn't stop the Richter family from expressing them anyway. A Bud and Julie hug became a father, mother and children hug, with Elsie standing to touch Bud's buttocks with her front paws.

"Anything else happen?"

"Someone threw rocks through Pete Lidell's windows."

"That's what he gets for helping me."

"What is it, Bud. What's going on?"

"It's all connected. I've had a thousand miles to think on it."

Julie and the kids followed him to the kitchen, where Bud immediately called the FBI in Denver, who called the Sterling motel room occupied by Agents Mosier and Petry, who phoned Bud within minutes.

"Bud Richter, this is Agent Ray Mosier."

"Ray, have you heard about what's happening here?"

"No. What?"

"Anarchy. That's what." Bud read off the list of events from Lisa's car to Pete's windows, and then dropped the name. "I suggest you focus your Herb Malik investigation on one man. Harold Turley."

"We're on our way to your place. Give us an hour."

Before any of his family members could ask, Bud dialed another number. "Helen, is Pete home?"

"No, he's at the store."

"Thank you."

"Bud, what's..."

Too late. Bud clicked off. "Where's the number for Pete's business?" Julie found it and read it to him. "Pete, this is Bud."

"Bud, are you home?"

"Yes."

"This damn town has gone crazy. I'm standing here with a shotgun protecting my store myself. Wes won't do shit to help me. Says kids did it. That's bullshit. Harold Turley did this and everybody knows it. If those mother fuckers come around here I'm gonna blast 'em."

"No, Pete. Don't do that. You stand your ground. Is Marvin there with you?"

"Yeah. I got him back in the dark so no one knows he's here. If they come, he's got his shotgun ready to go."

"If they come, just shoot to scare 'em. Don't kill anybody. You've got plywood back there. Board up your windows and wait. I've got the FBI coming. You just hold on until they get here."

"FBI? What are..."

Too late. Bud clicked off. "I'm starving. What've you got?"

Not only was he starving, his body was exhausted, but he didn't know it. Bud's adrenal glands worked overtime to keep him pumped up and waiting. He was halfway through his plate of warmed over ham steak when Agents Mosier and Petry arrived.

"Come on in, fellas," Bud greeted them on the front porch. "We've got coffee. Hell, Julie will cook for you if you're hungry."

They weren't, but they did drink her coffee. Everybody gathered in the kitchen, including Lisa and Jack. "They're mature," Bud explained to Ray Mosier's concern. "Nothing they can't handle."

"So, who is Harold Turley?"

Bud explained it all in between bites, the ongoing feud from World War II until the day Greg Dietrich ousted Turley's gang from his restaurant. Bud detailed every aspect of every event he could remember, several of which Jack and Lisa had heard only as rumors, several more of which they had never heard at all. Both agents listened without interrupting. Both were intrigued, but neither of them could make the connection to their case, the Herbert Malik investigation.

"Me neither," Bud admitted. "That is until those final miles to Cheyenne. One word kept popping into my head. A word Turley used that day he was kicked out. *Rag head,* that's your connection. Agent Petry, you remember that little trick you played on me? The one that pissed me off?"

"Yes."

"Try it on Turley. Try it on all of 'em. Those hayseeds will fall right into it. Might even go so far as to tell you everything you want to know, if they get angry enough."

"We're on it." Ray signaled for his partner to write. "Give us their names and addresses."

Bud listed the four men, and then called for them to return the favor. "We need help here. This town is on edge."

"It's coming from Denver. We'll pay a visit to Sheriff... what's his name?"

"Wes Harmon."

"...Sheriff Harmon to see if he needs any assistance. I'm sure that he will."

"Yeah, and he'll call his four buddies first chance he gets, too."

"I'm sure that he will, but I doubt if it's before his friends are in custody. Do you need a man out here?"

"Not if you arrest those four."

They were taken into custody, but they were expecting it. Pete had told his wife what Bud had told him, and from there the telephones rang nonstop, eventually reaching the wrong ears whose mouth got word to Sheriff Harmon. What Turley and his men had not anticipated was the questioning done individually in four separate rooms, which never touched on the subject of Greg Dietrich, but focused entirely on Herbert Malik. Each of them fell for Agent Petry's trick, but not to the degree hoped. Each spouted their diatribes of bigotry. None confessed to knowing a man named Herbert Malik.

As for Bud, Julie, Lisa and Jack, all four slept peacefully for the first night in several. Lisa and Jack would return to school on Wednesday, and while Bud and Julie would have preferred to take advantage of an entire house to themselves, they confined their sexual expressions to the turret bedroom. It was a precautionary measure taken in the likely event of interruption.

Sweet nothings had never been a part of the Julie and Bud love-making routine, and their Wednesday morning turret bedroom version was no exception. Bud told Julie sweet essentials and he told it all between kisses, between pokes from above. He told of Harry's demise, of Wally's sabotage, and of Harry's guidance to get Bud home. And with each new startling revelation, Julie clutched onto her husband with greater strength. She could not satisfy her desire for his closeness. She longed to meld his skin with hers, fuse his penis to her insides, until their moment of bliss was interrupted by way of Elsie's barking.

"It's them," naked Julie said from the window, as naked Bud laid on the bed.

"Another workout wasted. Let's welcome our guests with open arms, pretty titties and hard dick. Shall we?"

"Get dressed, Bud. I could strike a fancy to Agent Petry. But Mosier? Absolutely not."

The Secret Ingredient

"So, that Turley's a tough nut to crack, is he?"

"We can't connect any of them to Herbert, not yet." Ray Mosier sat on the porch swing looking a bit weathered. Petry stood with one hand leaning on a support column, more frustrated than bedraggled. Julie had fully dressed. Bud had only managed his usual gym shorts and sandals.

"Were you having another workout, Bud?"

"Why, John, what ever do you mean? Coffee, anyone?"

While Julie fetched, Bud talked mostly to Ray. "I suppose all four alibied one another for that Monday night."

"Of course. Are you sure about this, Bud?"

"No, damn it. I wish that sun hadn't been right in my eyes. We sat there waiting for two cars to pass north to south. I know one was a pickup, and I'd almost swear that the car was Turley's big old Lincoln. It was a four-door monster of some sort, but I can't be sure it was his."

"Well, that's not good enough."

"I know it. Hell, maybe I'm seeing things that aren't there."

"Well, they hate Arabs. You weren't wrong about that."

"They hate everybody who ain't them."

Julie returned with three mugs distributed to three men. "Bud, don't forget we need to go to Julesburg before the kids get home."

"Don't know, Julie. May not have time today."

"Bud Richter," Julie seriously admonished. "You *are* going to that hospital today. Maggie needs you there more than anybody else. Mark and Maggie both need to see you. I will drag you there by your ear if that's what I have to do."

"Sounds like you're going to Julesburg, Bud."

Mark, Greg, Maggie, the Kup, a connection, Bud got an idea.

"Ray, have you guys done your florensics on Herb?"

"Forensics," corrected smart-ass Petry.

"It's all in the lab now."

"What about the autopsy?"

"Ah, all fists, no weapons, official cause of death from internal bleeding. That may change to asphyxiation. They reckon Herbert might have still been alive when they buried him."

"How long can you hold them?"

"We've got them in Sterling now. They'll transfer to Phillips County for the crimes here when we're finished. I suppose I could hold them on Herbert's behalf about twenty-four hours. Make it around midnight."

"Call me here around five. I might have a connection for you."

"Bud, that's our dinner time. Call at six, please."

"Jesus Christ. We're trying to solve a murder and she's worried about dinner. Ok, call at six."

There was still time to finish their bed activities before leaving for the hospital, but it was more functional than romantic. Little was said on the trip to Julesburg, as Bud entertained by whistling -- the hyper-active variety, with an illogical and previously non-existent melody that's composed by a man whose brain is working on another project.

Maggie was there. Mark had gone to the smoking area for a cigarette. Greg laid atop hospital bed, breathing assisted, tubes draining organ blood.

"Oh, Bud," Maggie welcomed him, rising from her bedside chair with arms spread. "It's so good to see you."

Bud kissed her cheek, wrapped his arms beneath hers. "I am so sorry, Maggie. I should have stopped pestering them long ago."

"You didn't do anything wrong, Bud. If it wasn't for you they would have run over all of us long before now." She squeezed him tight. "Greg's sleeping now. Woke up with the sunrise, just like we were going to open the Kup." Tears streamed down her cheeks.

"So, he came out of the coma?"

"Yes, Bud." Maggie separated so she could peck Bud's lips. "First thing he said? He... he asked if my pies were ready for the oven. Can you believe it?"

"Well, of course. Where would he be without them?"

"Hello, Julie. Thanks for coming." Maggie broke away from him to embrace her. "Aren't men awful, Julie?"

"The bad ones are. You and I got the good ones."

"So, what do the doctors say?"

"He's going to make it, Bud. Eighty-percent chance, but it'll be a long process. They ruptured his spleen, kidneys and liver. Sound familiar?"

"Sure does. Gut-punching son of a bitch." Bud took Greg's hand, knelt down to bring his mouth to Greg's ear. "Don't you worry, Greg old buddy," he spoke in low volume, but at a level audible to Maggie and Julie. "Me and Maggie are gonna get him for murder, too. He'll be put away for a long, long time."

"What does he mean, Julie?"

"I don't know. His wheels have been turning ever since he got home."

"Bud? What are you talking about?"

"Well, I think Harold and his boys killed that FBI agent."

"The one who came to see you?"

"Right. My old Navy pal. You're the key to my idea, but I need my wife to give us some privacy before I can talk to you about it."

"I'll go find Mark," Julie cooperated. "See if I can cheer him up."

"Sit down, darlin'."

Maggie took her chair and Bud knelt before her, taking her hands in his. "Now, you know I would never betray you. Don't you?"

"Bud, get to the point. You're acting like you're going to propose for marriage, for goodness sakes."

"Over the years, how many times has Harold or any of them bought one of your pies?"

"Never. That day you had your argument... the day Greg kicked them out... that is the first time they've ever purchased food of any sort."

"That's what I figured."

"Why?"

"Maggie, whatever it is you put into those fruit pies, I need to know. I'm gonna tell it to the FBI agent. Nobody else."

"What are you talking about? I use whatever fruit, fresh, frozen or canned, and sugar, flour and butter. Everybody knows what goes into..."

"Wrong. You do something else. I know it. I'm no fool. I've tasted pies all over this country and..."

Greg mumbled the answer, causing Bud and Maggie to turn their heads. His eyes were still closed and he laid as though nothing had changed.

"Did you get that?" Maggie smiled.

"Got it." Bud rested his head on Maggie's lap. "It'll soon be over, sweetheart."

She ran fingers through his hair, fingertips along his back. "Sometimes I don't know whether I should be jealous of Julie or feel sorry for her."

"A little of both, I guess." Bud pulled away from her and stood. "I feel the same way about Greg." He moved towards her husband, kissed the stricken man on his forehead. "Maggie's waiting for you, Greg. We all are."

Julie and Mark entered, Mark receiving a hug from Bud rather than the traditional handshake. "Do you need anything?"

"No, I'm fine. Staying with mom until dad comes home. Then we'll figure out what to do. Got an extra house laying around somewhere?"

"Sorry, only got one big one. Were you insured?"

"Sure."

"That'll help."

"Oh, yeah. I'll rebuild right where I was, eventually."

"You call us, both of you. We'll be popping in here about every day until he's home."

No braggarts of idle promises, Bud and Julie did visit every day, Julie coming alone when Bud was on the road. The routine continued after Greg was released from the hospital. He was gifted home visits from the Richters until he was ready to join Maggie at his restaurant. After a two-week hiatus, Maggie Dietrich went back to work and The Koffee Kup Kafe resumed its tradition as best eatery on Main Street, its customers patiently accepting an abbreviated menu and longer waits for service. Mark helped when he could, but his kitchen career was a dead end. Never could match the technique and skill of his father, but everybody, customers and staff, did what they could to save the Kup.

Wednesday night after dinner, Jack was anxious to again ride his motorbike after four days of denial. Lisa, who had been banished from excessive phone use during her home imprisonment, her mother wishing to keep both lines open, was more than ready to make up for talking time lost on her private line.

As for the telephone itself, there was a ring on the main line just after six, but it was Perry Jacobs, not Ray Mosier.

"Bud?"

"Hello, Perry."

"How are things down there?"

"Mostly calm. The men causing the trouble are locked up for the time being."

"Are you gonna make it back on schedule? You know we're short-handed."

"Sunday late. That's my plan."

"Ok, just checking up on you. Making sure everybody's ok."

"I appreciate that. Hey, can I call you back in about half an hour. I'm expecting a call from the law."

"Sure, Bud."

"You at home?"

"Yeah."

"Talk to you later."

Julie's hands were in dishwater, as Bud resumed his duties of carting dirty items from table to kitchen counter. "You must have offended Agent Mosier. He hasn't called."

"Maybe they figured out something on their own. It is what they're trained to do."

"They can't do shit without me. You know that."

"Great. The truck driving detective. Now there's a title we can do without."

"Aren't you gonna ask me what my private conversation with Maggie was about?"

"Not going to give you that pleasure, Bud."

"What kind of pleasure are you going to..." The expected call came.

"Bud? Ray Mosier."

"Anything new?"

"No. Waiting on you."

"Turley wears his high school class ring all the time. Did you notice? Yeah, I know. Hard to believe, ain't it? Send it to your lab. I believe you will find a rather unique ingredient on that ring. Same goes for Herb's clothes. Bottom of his shirt, top of his jeans. And that ingredient is..." Bud turned away, cuffed the mouthpiece and whispered the word. "Got it?"

"Got it. Why the hush?"

"Becaaaaause, it's an old family recipe. If word got out, the Koffee Kup Kafe would be ruined."

"Oh, well we couldn't have that."

"We most certainly could not. Well, Ray, that's it. If that doesn't close the deal, I'm out of ideas."

"I'll let you know. Thank you, Bud."

Julie stood with hands dripping and firmly clamped to her hips, waiting for him to turn around. "Bud Richter, you *are* going to tell me Maggie's secret."

"Oh, *honey*, I can't tell you."

"It's honcy? I knew it."

"Oh, my precious *paprika*, my lips are sealed."

"Bud! What is it?"

"Darling *ginger*, sweet *rosemary*, voluptuous *vanilla*, please don't hurt me."

"Damn you." She found his tit beneath his shirt and twisted. "Tell me what it is."

"Nope. Gotta catch me first." Bud pulled away and streaked out the back door with Julie four steps behind. He stopped, grabbed her and took them both to the ground. After a few rolls down the slope and towards the fence, Julie and Bud came to a rest, laughing hysterically with Bud on top. "Insects are gonna eat us alive."

"It's spring," Julie sighed. "They've got other things to eat."

"Look. There's our pond. Wanna make another baby?"

"No."

"Wanna pretend like we're making another baby?"

"Later."

"It's not fair. You drive me nuts. Don't you know that?"

"I've had my suspicions."

"Let's go to bed."

"The kids are still up."

"They don't care. It probably turns their stomach, but they don't care."

"You're supposed to call Perry."

"Oh, that's right. Then can we go to bed?"

"Maybe."

"That's good enough for me. Come on, let's finish the kitchen."

She washed, he dried, and then he listened to the sad tale of Wally, who merely wanted to make Harry look bad but ended up killing him. No alcohol was necessary to pry the information out of Wally, although alcohol is what caused him to devise his foolish plan in the first place. Jealousy, greed and resentment fueled his determination to carry it out when sober. Bud was not the target. With two new tractors going on the road the same day, Wally didn't know which would be assigned to Harry, so he dropped his sand into both. Harry and another would earn a splotch on their driving records, perhaps perpetrate a minor collision. Their misfortune would bump them down the ladder, maybe even ground them indefinitely, allowing Wally to resume his place on the top rung through emergency need.

Foolish man. Never bothered to research the ramifications of gritty sand working its way amongst the gears of a hard-working transmission mile after mile. Never considered that a transmission might do anything other than slip, giving its driver ample warning that something was wrong. A transmission suddenly locking up never entered his head. Worst of all, Wally never considered the possibility of any person dying from his selfishness. Wally just wanted his job back. Lucky for him only one man died. Had it not been for Harry's skills and compassion, there could have been many.

"Rotten way to show gratitude, ain't it, Perry."

"Yeah. I should have just fired him and been done with it. What the hell, sometimes you take a chance on a man and it backfires. That's rare, though. Most times the man will reward you... somewhere down the road."

"Like Robert?"

"Hey, he's doing great. Clearing out two trailers a night."

"Told you. Maybe you oughtta think about making him a driver."

"Already have thought about it. Just a matter of time."

"Time's all he needs... and encouragement. Well, Perry, let's put this behind us. You can't always be right."

"Yeah, I'm trying to move forward. Just wanted to make sure my A number one driver is ok."

"He is. He's about to boink his wife. How's that sound?"

"Sounds like Bud. See you on Sunday."

"Thanks for calling, Perry."

Julie had showered and was working on her hair when Bud entered to wash away his yard itch, too. Together, they lightly tapped on Lisa's door, telling her they were going to bed early. She said goodnight, and then told her phone friend that her mom and dad were going to slobber all over each other. "It's so disgusting. Actually, I think it's kind of sweet. Margie says her parents get in their hot tub after they think she's asleep and do it in there. Isn't that just sick?"

"Hmm... Mrs. Richter, perhaps we should investigate this hot tub business."

Man on the Altar

Ring to finger, finger to fist, fist to shirt stained with pie filling all connected to foil the Turley gang. Agents Mosier and Petry smartly presented this revelation to the four men in the same room at the same time, and naturally, one of them turned on Harold to save himself a few years of prison time.

Bud was right about the secret ingredient, but wrong about it all being over. The brains of the offspring had already been tainted with the same ignorance as the parents, and so they hated without knowing why. Unlike those boys, Jack would learn useful information from his father, like the sweet science of boxing, which was necessary after two boys jumped Jack on the school grounds. The next fall, next school year, they tried it again with results dramatically reversed.

While Ronnie Stover was blathering on about what Harold and the other two did, Bud and Julie were lost in each other, fondling, kissing and inspecting Bud's fur-covered belly scar where Harold's ring had imprinted him years earlier. Julie's licking made it all better. She toyed with her ammunition -- Maggie's secret ingredient, in preparation for when the house was theirs.

"You will talk."

"Think so?"

"I'll put you on the bench."

"Promise?"

"Then, we'll see how tough you are."

"I am."

In reality, the Bud-built bench in the basement was not for punishment purposes, but for reward. It provided discomfort to a small degree, mainly because the victim's back was made to arch upwards, his legs spread apart and dangling on either side, his wrists parallel with his ears and pulled towards the floor. Bud was strong enough to take it, and for Julie, her man was presented to her in a glorious display of masculine beauty. Next morning, with the kids at school, she took him there.

His chest rose high into the air, his belly flattened, his lines of muscle handsomely defined. Positioned perfectly near one end of the bench, his penis and balls were elevated, isolated and obtainable. She could stand directly above them and do with them as she pleased -- her very special, all-consuming oral expertise, but for this he would be forced to wait.

She quickly abandoned her questioning for the ingredient, instead praising him for all his good deeds, his fathering, his crime-solving, his devotion to her. Julie worshiped her man on the altar with words and fingers and lips and tongue, put to skin and fur and tits and muscle until she could no longer deny him. Unable to further tolerate the incessant bobbing of his unattended penis, she drained him Julie style.

"Bud, is it too late to start a garden?" She casually questioned as she untied his wrists and ankles. "It depresses me to see those old jars on the shelf... the ones your mother canned."

"Mother? Probably grandmother, too." He raised his arm to her. "Pull me up."

"You didn't answer my question." She took his hand and tugged him to sit. "Can I have a garden?"

"Vegetable? Flower? What?"

"Maybe both."

"Do you know how?"

"Well, I can read, can't I? Perhaps I'll just ask your mother how to do it."

"Right. Good luck."

"You never know. Let's go see her and find out."

The nursing home complex was built as individual apartments east of downtown Holyoke. Coaxing Bud to stop at a market, Julie purchased a flower arrangement which would look pretty for a day or two and placed it on the table by a window where Bud's mother sat in a chair. One of her attending staff had angled the chair so that she could look out the window, but her eyes were fixed to the wall below.

Bud and Julie, mostly Julie, spoke to her as though she knew what was being said. Told her about Lisa and Jack, about their school activities, about Jack's new motorcycle helmet, about Lisa's new hood locks and alarm for her auto. And when Bud grew uncomfortable, which was quickly, he spoke as though his mother was not there.

"Hey, wanna try out her bed?"

"Bud, stop it."

"You gonna ask her about the garden or what?"

"Clara, Bud wants me to start a garden. He thought you might have some tips for me." Julie leaned close and listened. "Uh huh... ok... I'll do that."

"Did you get some useful information?"

"Yes, Bud."

"Good. Let's go." He kissed the woman on her cheek. "Bye,

mom."

Julie repeated Bud's move and followed him to the door, but as Bud exited and continued to the car, Julie turned to retrace her steps. She took a cut daffodil from the flower arrangement and threaded its stem through the woman's fingers. "Thank you, Clara Richter." She kissed the woman's dribbling mouth. "Thank you for your son."

Like the gut of Greg Dietrich, and before that Bud Richter, the town of Holyoke was bruised but not defeated. Holyoke was reborn. A long-festering cycle of hatred had ended. Another generation of conflict awaited its future. But for now, there was relief. A part-time resident had restored calm. Bud's protectors were a powerful force, and the good people of Holyoke were benefactors of that force.

Pete Lidell and his helper Marvin were installing new glass windows, and Bud pulled a sudden move to grab a parking space in front.

"What are you doing?"

"I need to place an order with Pete."

"What is it?"

"I worked up an estimate for the paint we'll need to cover Jack's barn. Wanna help me pick out a color?"

"Shouldn't Jack do that?"

"No. You and I remember the old red, or what was left of it. Come on."

While there, Bud decided it was time for Lisa to upgrade her car stereo from eight-track to cassette, and Pete was thankful for that purchase plus the down payment to order many gallons of brickyard red exterior paint, due to arrive within three business days.

"I'll need white for the trim, but we'll get that when I pick up the red."

"Want me to deliver it for you?"

"No thanks, Pete. That's what my wagon's for. Keep my cans dry and dirt-free."

When Bud and Julie passed by the Kup, Mark was inside, and upon seeing Bud's wagon he streaked out to flag him down. Julie came inside, too.

"Here. Maggie made this for you."

"Blackberry?"

"What else?"

"How did she find the time to do this? What a sweetheart."

"Dad told her to. She would've anyway. After all you've done. Hell, the entire town's making stuff for you guys. Look at this."

Lined along the working counter in the back kitchen were all kinds of home-baked items -- cakes, cookies and cobblers numbering over a dozen. Taped to each were handwritten notes of gratitude to Bud and Julie.

"How are we supposed to eat all of this?"

"Oh, Bud," Julie chided. "It's the thought that counts."

"Well, they thought too hard. I hope Elsie is hungry."

As Julie carted the items to Bud's wagon, he looked around the abandoned restaurant, tables and chairs covered with six days of dust, illuminated only by window-streaked sunlight. "Are you getting things cleared out, Mark?"

"No, getting things cleaned up. Mom wants to open up next week."

"Hey, that's great news. Your dad must be healing up quick."

"It'll be a few weeks until he can come home, but he wants mom to at least do the breakfast crowd. I'm going to help her best I can."

"Well, we're headed to Julesburg right now to see him. I'm sure we will hear all about it."

"Yeah, Bud. You keep quiet and let him talk for a change. It'll do him good."

"Sure will, Mark. Good to see you working hard."

At the four-way stop sign of decision, Bud asked. "Should we take the desserts home first or go to the hospital first?"

"We're taking the desserts to the nursing home, and then we're going to the hospital."

"Aw, not my blackberry."

"No, Bud. We're keeping the Maggie pie."

"Damn right we are. And while I'm eating that you can write thank you's to everybody who tried to fatten me up with their inferior products."

"Ingrate."

Bud turned around to retrace his path. With all goodies except for Maggie's delivered to the nursing home office, Bud and Julie took one more trip down Main Street, turning right on the 385 for Julesburg.

"Bud, after we see Greg and Maggie, let's go to the Super-Mart and look at hot tubs."

"Hell, no. We'll order one from Pete, if you want one."

"Can't we just look?"

"No, because you'll want to buy. Hey, Jack and I will design a private place in the barn for us to play in it."

"Poor Jack."

"Poor Jack nothing... poor me. Mmm... water torture."

"Turn around and go to Pete's. Right now."

Old pain washed in new red paint. Broken boards replaced by new boards of pleasure. Finally on the road to Julesburg, en route to visit the Dietrichs, Bud produced a fork stolen from the Kup.

"Give me my pie."

With Julie feeding him, Bud drove with left hand on the wheel, right hand on the V of her jeans. Bud Richter savored the sweet taste of Maggie blackberry, as he clutched onto the juicy woman he could never let go.

About the Author

You might know Jasper from his audio series, Uncle Jasper's Five-fingered Bedtime Stories, available as Podcasts or downloadable as audio MP3's from his nephew's web site, Jardonn's Erotic Tales.com. Jasper's tales, both audio and written are derived from the many people he has met through the years, working-class nobodies like himself who strive to get by month to month while enjoying life to its fullest.

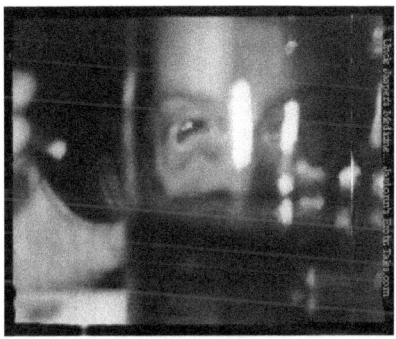